WORSHIPED

EMMA SHELFORD

WORSHIPED

Kinglet Books
Victoria BC, Canada

Cover design by Deranged Doctor Designs

ISBN: 978-1989677278 (print)
ISBN: 978-1989677254 (ebook)

www.emmashelford.com

First edition: November 2020

CHAPTER I

I idly twirl a strand of energy through the air while I watch Minnie do a downward dog and read her phone. It's quite a talent to do both at the same time.

"Listen to this." Minnie's voice is muffled from her shirt pooling around her mouth. She drops to her knees and shakes her brown hair out of her face. "There's some woman in town styling herself as the prophet of the Aztec earth goddess Coatlicue. Says the second coming is nigh." She looks at me with a grin. "Who knew it was the Aztecs who had it right after all?"

"I wish I'd visited them at their zenith." I stand and pull strands of energy, those I call lauvan, from around the couch. If I balance cushions on the armrests, their precarious position will give them enough potential energy for me to manipulate. My fingers work with swift motions. "They sounded fascinating, human sacrifices notwithstanding. I was ricocheting between Africa and Europe at the time, and the Spanish were only beginning to dream of traveling that far."

"What a weird choice." Minnie peruses the article again while I work. "Old Aztec gods. I presume the woman has a history of mental illness, otherwise she would more likely be fanatical about the religion she was raised with, not a distant, half-forgotten culture."

I make the final tweak to my project. The couch vanishes and is replaced by an ornate wooden chair carved in a style that matches my scanty knowledge of Aztec symbolism. I bow with a flourish.

"Your throne, my lady." I wave at Minnie to sit. "I may not speak with the gods, but you will always be my queen."

Minnie giggles and stands. She curtseys to me then lowers

herself onto the throne.

"Not the coziest contraption." She wiggles to get comfortable. "I wonder if the real ones had cushions."

"Most assuredly." I twist the strands of the coffee table until a matching throne appears. I sit and drape my legs over the armrest then grin at Minnie. "Now we can rule from our thrones together forever."

"At least until I die." Minnie traces the carving of her throne. She smiles at me. "Then you can rule with the reborn version of me."

Flashes of memory assault me. Nimue dying, Gretchen dying, Khutulun dying, Celeste dying… I shake my head to rid it of the recollections. I have lived for centuries, and although I didn't know it was her, my first love Nimue was reborn after she died and came back to me as many different women. I fell in love with each one in turn then endured fourteen heart-wrenching deaths of my beloveds until I met Minnie and discovered that she and my other friends—Arthur, Guinevere, Gawaine—came back to me every time they were reborn.

I push the morbid thoughts away. There is no use dwelling on past tragedy, not when my living, breathing fiancée is within my grasp. I smile when a thought occurs to me.

"Don't forget, you're different this time, a half-elemental like me." We both had fathers possessed by elemental spirits from a parallel plane of existence. Even I have trouble wrapping my head around it sometimes. "You'll probably live longer this time. I've been around for fifteen hundred years and am still going strong."

"True." Minnie looks thoughtful. "You've been thirty for centuries. I admit, not aging is appealing. I was dreading the thought of my first gray hair. But will I live as long as you? I thought earth elementals lasted far longer than others. My affiliation is water."

"The second longest-lasting," I say firmly. "You will be with me for a long time yet. I'm looking forward to it."

My eyes must still be haunted by memories of her deaths, for she reaches forward with a look of understanding and runs her hand through my black hair, cut short for this time.

"Enjoy the days as they come, Merlin," she says in Brythonic, my mother tongue. The adage makes my heart swell, and I spontaneously press my lips to hers. When we part, Minnie sits back with a gleam in her eye.

"We need to talk," she says.

"Uh oh. That rarely starts a conversation I like."

She waves my concern away.

"Our wedding. When are we going to bite the bullet? It's not like we're planning the event of the year. A visit to city hall won't take long."

My stomach turns at the thought of planning for the future. It's too soon after discussing Minnie's many deaths. I need to separate those events in my mind. Despite my hope for a longer future with this incarnation of my love due to her half-elemental status, the fear always lurks. I want to enjoy the days as they come, not stare at a future that only marches toward death.

"Sometime," I say evasively. "We'll make it happen soon."

"How about tomorrow?"

I look at Minnie in shock, and her eyes twinkle in merriment.

"We could, I suppose. Is there anything to arrange?"

"It's all taken care of," she says and kisses my forehead. "Just show up in a suit."

"You've been planning this for a while, haven't you?" I say in defeat. Minnie chuckles and stands.

"Somebody had to."

Minnie walks to the kitchen, and a moment later the sound of running water emerges from the doorway. I slump into my

3

throne. Now that Minnie is out of sight, the malaise that rears its ugly head when she's not with me takes over. I don't understand my dissatisfaction. I have everything I ever wanted—my friends returned to me, my lover by my side, the promise of a cheerful future—so what am I yearning for?

I glance up when I feel eyes on me. Minnie sips a glass of water and stares at me with concern.

"What's wrong?" she asks. "You're mopey again."

"I'm tired of being an instructor of English literature." I pick the reason at whim, although it's true that I don't feel the same zest for teaching as I used to. "Perhaps it's time for a switch in career."

Minnie nods slowly.

"Maybe. What are you thinking of next?"

I raise my palms in a gesture of helplessness.

"I have no idea."

"I'll print off some personality tests that I use for my clients. Maybe they can help you narrow down your next choice."

"You truly think I don't know myself by now?" I stare at Minnie with amusement. "I've had too many years to plumb the depths of my soul."

"Sometimes it helps to have an outside look." Minnie steps toward me and kisses me on the cheek. "Get an objective opinion on how to find your direction in life."

I don't know that I need direction. I waited centuries for Arthur to return—it was the one true goal that kept me pushing onward through my endless, seemingly pointless life—and now he's here, along with Nimue and the others, I should be basking in a job well done. What prevents me from that satisfaction?

October rain pours down relentlessly, but it doesn't dampen Minnie's spirits.

"It's good luck to have rain on our wedding day."

She squeezes my hand as we walk toward city hall. I pull our shared umbrella closer to our heads to avoid damp on Minnie's carefully curled hair.

"I think that was made up by a disappointed bride. Unless it refers to the symbolism of rain bringing fertile crops."

"That's probably it." She glances at me. "We're not going to go there again, are we?"

In our many years together, we have had three children, but none survived past their fourth year. I shake my head tightly.

"I'd rather not go through that loss again. You are welcome to convince me otherwise, but my first reaction is no."

Minnie nods and slips her fingers out of mine. The sense of loss is palpable until she tucks her hand into the crook of my arm and nestles closer as we walk.

"I hear you," she says.

We walk in comfortable silence, both lost in our own thoughts, until Minnie points to a telephone pole covered in posters. I stop to look at what caught her attention.

"It's that woman I was telling you about," she says. "The one claiming to be the second coming of that Aztec goddess."

"Is she recruiting via posters now?" I chuckle and peer closer. The poster is stylized with a vintage look, and in the center is an illustration of a woman wearing a blouse and long skirt with a headdress of woven branches on her head. Her arms are raised in supplication, or perhaps to show her might. I squint at the face, hardly daring to guess.

"Look," I say hoarsely. "Who do you think that looks like?"

Minnie stares for a moment, then her breath hisses with a gasp.

"March Feynman," she breathes. "What is she doing?"

"What is Xenia doing, you mean," I say grimly. The elemental Xenia currently possesses the body of March Feynman, a local businesswoman who was determined to bring the power of the elementals to Earth. She succeeded, to her detriment, for the ruling earth elemental, the fundamental herself, now resides in March's body. She calls herself Xenia, and I hoped we had seen the last of her after her defeat at our hands a few weeks ago.

"Coatlicue," Minnie says slowly. "Primordial earth goddess. What is Xenia's game?"

"She wants to be worshiped?" I stare at the poster again. "I suppose being cooped up in dormancy really did a number on her ego. While she's on Earth, she wants to feel some love from the humans, since her elemental compatriots weren't giving her any."

"Do you think it's that benign?" Minnie asks.

I scoff.

"Her skirt is sewn with shells, and she has a bundle of sticks on her head. How could anyone take her seriously? If she manages to attract followers, more the fool them."

"She could show some earth moves. Miracles, you know. That might convince some."

"Still, what does she truly gain from it? A bit of an ego boost, that's all. Honestly, this is the most harmless thing I can think of that Xenia could get up to. If she wants to start a following, it's vastly better than the alternatives. With her power, she could sink islands or level mountains, not to mention the murdering she was engaging in earlier. A little worship singing is the least of our worries."

"I guess." Minnie doesn't look convinced, but I squeeze her arm and pull her in the direction of city hall again.

"We'll keep an eye on the situation. At least now we know

6

where she is. We can track her easily enough if she's passing out fliers advertising her whereabouts." Although a twinge of unease lances through me at the sight of March's face lifted in exultation, I push it aside. "Come, don't let Xenia ruin our special day. After all, we only get to do this a dozen or so times."

City hall looms ahead, its blocky white clock tower ten floors high at the peak and dropping down in steps from there. A few trees attempt to soften the squareness. I grow quiet when we approach the cement steps rising between lamp posts. Previous weddings flit through my mind, the memories bittersweet. Some were ostentatious pageants designed for splendor, and some were quiet, moonlit affairs with nothing but a priest and a ring. All were with Minnie.

"Do you remember when you married me as Edith in Francia?" Minnie says quietly. Her mind must be following the same path as mine. "It was a handfast ceremony. A twist of fabric, a few words, and we were married. Simple, but beautiful."

I laugh.

"Compare it to Zanetta's Italian extravaganza."

"Night and day."

We reach the doors where Alejandro and Jen wait for us beside a plump, middle-aged woman with a jovial face. I glance at Minnie and she grins.

"You planned everything, didn't you?" I say. "Witnesses and an officiant waiting for us."

"Somebody had to."

Alejandro claps me on the back and Jen exchanges hugs with

7

Minnie, then I push the doors open for Minnie and the others.

A few signed papers and ten minutes under a tree in the plaza outside, then the deed is done. Minnie waves her left hand at me where a gold band gleams on the finger I recently slid it on.

"I'm a missus again," she says with a laugh. "My friends think I'm crazy, by the way, getting married so soon. It's a bit hard to explain without using words like soulmate that make people roll their eyes."

I look contentedly at my own band, unadorned yet signifying the endless loop of our unity. This is where I belong, with Minnie, always. I am meant to be by her side. It's my place, and I feel light and complete again with the renewal of our commitment to each other. Minnie is back for good, with full knowledge of our history, and she is mine again for the fifteenth time. Nothing can get in the way of our happiness now.

Xenia's poster snakes through my mind, but I banish the thought by looking at Minnie's beaming face. Xenia has no place on this special day.

"You're mine once again." I twirl her around in a circle while she gasps, then I cover her mouth with a deep kiss. Minnie pushes me away with a playful smack on the chest.

"Behave, husband, or I'll have to show you who's boss."

"Is that a promise?"

The comment earns me another smack and a giggle.

Minnie leads me, Jen, and Alejandro to a nearby Indian restaurant. Inside, a corner of the room is our clear destination. It's festooned with balloons and streamers, the latter of which remind me irresistibly of lauvan. Wayne, Anna, Liam, and Cecil are seated at the pushed-together tables, and at the sight of us, they erupt in a loud cheer that has the other customers craning their necks to see what's happening. Minnie waves and pulls me forward.

8

"Congratulations," Wayne says when he jumps up and squeezes me around the shoulder. The burn scars on his face twist with his broad smile. "You finally found each other again."

The rest stand to greet us, and the next few minutes are a whirl of hugs and boisterous congratulations. I eventually usher my friends into their seats after a few pointed glances from the servers.

Once we are seated, chatter breaks out and menus open. Jen leans toward me.

"I've been meaning to ask you. Whatever happened to that police officer who was after you? You know, the one at the battle who let us go?"

Wayne chuckles from across the table.

"Kat didn't learn about elementals gracefully."

"Officer Lee sat down with Wayne and me," I say with a grateful swig of beer that a server places before me. "Mmm, that's what I wanted. The good officer maintained such a look of incredulity through our explanation that I thought her eyebrows would disappear into her hairline."

Jen's laugh makes bubbles in her margarita, and she grabs her napkin to clean up the resulting mess. I chuckle.

"I did, of course, give her a demonstration of my abilities."

"What trick did you do for her?" Liam asks from the end of the table.

"A three-part act for the skeptic. Levitation of her coffee, localized windstorm in her hair, and a redesign of Wayne's nose."

"Think Pinocchio," Wayne says with a grin. Cecil snorts.

"It all worked out." I lean back in my chair. "She turned a delicate shade of green and said she would forget everything in exchange for me keeping a low profile. I thought that was fair."

9

"It will be a difficult task," says Minnie. She pats my hand fondly. "But I know you'll try your best."

The others laugh, and we order our food. Alejandro stands again once the servers have retreated to the kitchen.

"Before we eat," he says. "I want to say some words. I've done this a few times before, so I have some practice." He grins at me. Alejandro has indeed been a close friend at many of my previous weddings. He clears his throat. "I wanted to say," he says in Brythonic. "Wait, that's not right," he says in Spanish. "Is it this?" he says in Swedish.

Everyone laughs and Alejandro grins widely. I chuckle, but Liam's face catches my eye. He doesn't look sad or concerned at this reminder of Alejandro's past, but instead he appears resolved. I wonder if he has come to a decision on whether to touch the grail and discover if he has a past. I will have to ask him about it later.

"But seriously," Alejandro continues in English. "I am so pleased that you two have found each other again, and that I am here to witness it and understand how important this moment is." He raises his glass. "To my oldest friend, Merry, and his wonderful wife, Minnie."

The rest raise their glasses and drink. Minnie stands once Alejandro sits.

"Thank you, Alejandro. And thank you all for being in our lives, in so many ways and through so many years. We are lucky to have each one of you."

"I agree." I rise and hold up my glass. "To long-standing friends and faithful lovers, and the happiness only they can bring."

The food is plentiful and the wine more so. We talk and laugh and cause more than one patron to glance our way in disapproval, but I don't care. Tonight is the most complete I have felt at a wedding since I married Nimue, centuries ago, and I revel in the feeling.

It's late by the time we stumble out of the restaurant, shouting goodbyes to our friends. I wave at a taxi and it miraculously stops for us. Minnie slurs out our address before collapsing on the seat and dragging me inside. I fall into her, and we both chuckle until we can control ourselves once more. The taxi driver raises his eyebrows.

"Good night?" he asks.

"We got married," Minnie blurts out and shows him her hand. The man whistles.

"Congrats, happy couple. You're a lucky man."

"The luckiest," I say and run my hand up Minnie's leg. She giggles, and the driver veers into traffic.

"It's been a busy night," the driver says in conversation, and I groan inwardly. Why is he making small talk, when clearly our minds are on other things?

"Has it?" Minnie says. She swats my hand away.

"For sure. Big night around the world. Of course, not as big as getting married." He grins in the rearview mirror, then his face turns serious. "Not so good for some, though. That typhoon that hit the coast of China today, that was rough. And bushfires in Australia are burning up the countryside. Tough go over there."

Minnie gamely engages his chatter while fending off my surreptitious advances. She has varying degrees of success keeping a smile off her face.

When we finally arrive at our apartment, I shove bills over the seat and pull Minnie out of the door to the driver's surprised farewell.

"Why didn't we fly home?" I ask Minnie. "It would have been far quicker, and we wouldn't have had to endure the chatterbox back there."

"In your state? You drunken fool. We would have smacked into the side of a building." Minnie mimes the action with her hands and makes a crashing sound with her mouth. The thought of the carnage that would have almost certainly occurred sends us both into paroxysms of laughter.

The elevator is an excuse for the kisses that I didn't get in the taxi. At our door, I sweep Minnie off her feet and carry her over the threshold. The grand gesture lasts until I stumble over my own feet, swing her around wildly, and end up on my bottom. A split second later, Minnie lands on my lap with a startled expression and forces all the air out of my lungs.

After we recover, I walk to the kitchen and pull a couple of beers out of the fridge. Minnie is already on the balcony, her heels kicked off and her feet on the railing. She rolls her eyes at the bottle I pass her.

"Because we need a little more alcohol," she says but reaches for the beer.

I settle in my chair and watch the few stars that are visible through patchy clouds that whisk across the sky in ragged streams. The rainstorm earlier has cleared, but a brisk wind took its place, and the biting cold promises wintery weather to come.

"Those are the same stars that we watched on the night you married me as Isabella in eleventh century Spain," Minnie says quietly. "They don't change, not ever. And my love for you doesn't change, either. Can eternal love be a real thing?"

"I think what we have is as close as one can get." I reach out my hand and run the backs of my fingers over her cheek in a gentle caress. "More than most will ever know." I take a swig of my beer. "You're feeling rather deep tonight."

12

"Maybe I have more than a thimbleful of emotional range," she snaps.

I can only blink in surprise. Where did that come from? My comment was no more than what she can expect from me, and she knows better than most the inaccuracy of her accusation.

Minnie runs a hand over her face and takes a deep breath.

"I'm sorry," she says through closed eyes. "That wasn't necessary."

"Are you still feeling the other personality?" I ask quietly. Ever since she uncovered her heritage and abilities, she has had trouble controlling her elemental side, and it sometimes comes out in ways she doesn't intend.

"I'm trying to control it, but it's not always easy." She sighs again and holds out her hand. "Forgive me?"

"Always," I say and take her fingers in my own. "If you're feeling better, I could prove it."

Minnie's smile turns coy. She gets up with only the slightest sway and straddles my legs. Her lips brush mine with a featherlight touch.

"Convince me," she says.

My hands caress her thighs, and she sighs in anticipation. Our strands twine together as her hips move against my lap in sultry circles, and I press my lips against her silky neck. We are husband and wife on paper, but now I want to make her mine the old-fashioned way. I'm never a modern man.

"Challenge accepted."

CHAPTER II

Dreaming

I love a good party as much as the next lord, but this celebration is absurdity wrapped in a pastry of ostentation with a dab of ridiculousness smeared on top. From the troupes of jugglers and the barrels upon barrels of wine, to the dozens of courses of delicacies I have rarely tasted even in my long life and the towering sculptures of swans crafted of merengue from hundreds of eggs, the whole wedding feast was a spectacle worthy of a Renaissance princess.

Zanetta is neither a princess nor a particularly well-placed noble. Instead, she is the daughter of a Venetian merchant who has been fortunate in business of late and wishes to announce his new wealth to the world. What better way than to throw a wedding of such magnificence that the entire city will speak of it for weeks?

I, as Count Merlo di Noto of Rome and Zanetta's new husband, am also a cause for celebration in this merchant class family. It took a few years to establish myself in Rome—papers forged, the right people's strands manipulated to plant false memories, the purchase of an appropriate estate—but it was well worth it. I wanted to live like a prince for a while, and I had everything except a beautiful woman to share it with. It was hard to move on from Maria, but I managed eventually.

Then I met Zanetta, and everything changed again.

"When can we leave?" Zanetta whispers to me, her breath hot and sweet against my ear. Acrobats flip in front of us, and I suppress a shiver of longing at Zanetta's closeness.

"We must be seen off, I suppose." I look around at the guests, many of whom are falling over in their chairs from their

14

inebriation. "I could insist on it now."

"Please." Zanetta squeezes my hand under the table. "I grow weary of being on display. This is Papa's party, anyway. We were only an excuse."

I nod decisively and wave at a servant nearby. The man hurries over.

"Inform Señor Tonino that we will retire now, if he wishes to make any formal send-off."

The man nods and trots to Zanetta's father, whose red-faced cheer is infectious among his compatriots. The only reason I agreed to this farcical event was for this good-natured man, whose simple enjoyment of life and desire to see his family respected despite their lowly beginnings struck a chord in me.

Tonino looks at us with bloodshot eyes when the servant whispers in his ear, then he glances around the banquet room. Raucous laughter and shouts of merriment ring through the grand space. Even if he wanted to make a scene, it would be a feat to gather attention for it.

Tonino must come to the same conclusion, for he waves at us to leave. Zanetta needs no further encouragement. With startling speed, she leaps up and pulls my arm with vigor. We stumble away from the table and into the blissfully cool and calm hallway, our feet none too steady after an evening's frivolity.

"Finally," Zanetta moans with relief. "That was a test of endurance. This bodice is too tight to wear for much longer." She looks at me from under her lashes. "Perhaps you could help me take it off, dear husband."

I slowly slide my hands around her waist.

"Of course, my darling wife." I draw her close and lean in for a kiss. Before our lips meet, I bend and sling her over my shoulder in an avalanche of skirts.

She shrieks and beats at my back. She can barely push words

15

out through her laughter.

"Get me down, you brute!"

I grin and move with long strides to our nuptial chambers. When we reach the room, I kick the door ajar with my foot and pace through. It slams shut behind me, and I lay Zanetta on the huge four poster bed spread with a rich velvet coverlet. She is red-faced and panting with mirth.

"Come here, you ridiculous man," she breathes, then clutches the ruffles of my shirt and pulls me down for a kiss.

Braulio adjust my bowtie then smacks my face.

"What was that for?" I rub my cheek and stare at him, perplexed. He doesn't look the least bit apologetic.

"It's for good luck," he says. "Start your wedding day with a measure of pain, then the day will end with a measure of pleasure." At my disbelieving stare, he says, "Ancient tradition."

"I doubt that very much. But when it's your wedding day, expect retaliation."

"You'll be waiting a while," Braulio says with a laugh. "Marriage is for old men like you. I still have too much living to be tied to a woman."

"Perhaps you haven't met the right one yet." I look in the mirror of my hotel bathroom and smooth my hair into place with pomade. "Trust me, I know a little about getting married."

"Like I said. Old man." Braulio takes a brief glance in the mirror then pulls me away. "Stop preening. Josie is waiting."

At the thought of Josephine, I eagerly follow Braulio outside. He managed to procure a car—beg, borrow, or steal, I didn't enquire which, all I know is that he took a wad of cash from my wallet to pay for it—and it sits in rounded glory, gleaming with chrome and shiny enough to see my face in.

"Come on," Braulio urges. "Josie and her sister will be at the chapel before us at this rate. The bride is supposed to be the late one. We're lucky her sister agreed to come at all. Remember her scowl when she arrived?"

"She wasn't keen on our secret wedding."

I slide into the driver's seat. Braulio frowns at me.

"I thought I was driving."

I laugh in his face.

"Over my dead body. You're a terrible driver, and this car is too pretty to risk. Come on, now who's holding us up?"

We have to roust the minister out of his office for the ceremony, but he finally wiggles into his cassock and stands at the altar before us. The tiny Baptist chapel is empty, but a hired pianist plays *Prelude in C* by Bach when the chapel door opens and Josephine's sister Audrey walks down the aisle. She carries a bouquet of spring wildflowers hastily gathered this morning by the roadside. Her face, now that she is resigned to our rapid, unannounced wedding, wears a serene smile that reflects Josephine's own beauty.

When Audrey reaches us, she gives me a long stare then smiles. She takes her place across from Braulio, who gives her a wink which she ignores, and the music changes.

Josephine stands at the door, silhouetted against the brilliant sun of a Georgian spring morning. She wears a calf-length, cream-colored dress with a boat neck and a cinched middle that accentuates her slender waist. She is stunning, and my heart fills with more love than I thought it could ever hold.

She walks with measured steps down the aisle then gives her own spring bouquet to her sister and takes my hands in both of her own.

"Hi there, stranger," she says in her Southern drawl

accompanied by a sparkle in her blue eyes. "It's time you made an honest woman out of me."

CHAPTER III

Minnie has an early client this morning, but before she left, she extracted papers from her work bag and slid them onto the dining room table.

"Try these while I'm out," she said. "I know you think they're bogus but humor me. And look through that book."

I flip through the pages of the book after the door clicks shut. It's called *Finding Your Purpose* by Dr. Anish Vasu, and while the good doctor may have a wonderful bedside manner, his writing style is drier than the Sahara.

He does mention to imagine the purpose of others around oneself. Minnie adores her work and wants to make a difference in her clients' quality of life. What about the others? Alejandro enjoys his work as an English-as-a-second-language teacher, but he doesn't strike me as being terribly fulfilled in that role. Do his past lives have something in common? My mind drifts through his previous personalities, looking for common threads. Arnost helped orphans of the Black Plague, and Axel worked tirelessly to allow lower class boys to receive opportunities and education. What's the common ground there?

I shake my head and turn to the sheets of paper Minnie left me. There are multiple versions of different personality and career tests with pages upon pages of multiple-choice questions to fill out. I almost throw them aside in disgust, but Minnie's admonishments fill my mind. I pull them toward me with a sigh. Minnie even thoughtfully left a pencil at the ready. I sigh again, filling my lungs before exhaling forcefully, then get to work.

Some of the questions are obvious—*Do you feel more invigorated being with others or being alone*— and I check

19

boxes without thinking. Others cover the same concepts in different ways, and I snort at the mindless cretins who take these things in earnestness. I stumble on a few questions, but hastily circle an answer before I think too hard about it. I'm not in the mood for lengthy introspection right now.

I tally up the results and read my personality type.

Your personality is charming and attractive, and you love to explore and experience new things. You're a balanced mix of creative and down-to-earth, but don't forget to work on emotional sensitivity to succeed in relationships and careers. You chafe at being a subordinate with rules and regulations thrust upon you, so find a role that will use your experimentation and quick-thinking. When you find the right fit, you will throw yourself into it: work hard, play hard is your motto.

It goes on in excessive detail about work and relationships, but I snort with laughter and toss the test aside. It doesn't tell me anything I don't already know, except for an apparent penchant for risk-taking—perhaps I take a few risks, but long-term consequences are never far from my mind when all I have is the long term—and I don't know what I'm supposed to conclude. Should I be a paramedic or police officer since I am good at analyzing situations at a glance and acting on them? Perhaps Minnie will have some insight into my results, but I doubt it. I will decide my next career path the way I always do—try things until something sticks for a few years.

Besides, it doesn't matter what I do for work. My reason for surviving for the past fifteen hundred years was for the return of Arthur, and now he and the others are here. Minnie is my wife again, and I don't seek anything more. I am unbelievably lucky that she showed up and that the grail was there to reveal her true self. Most others never see their dreams come true.

Work is a way to pass the time, nothing more. If I'm bored

of teaching, I can switch to something else. Perhaps an airline pilot for the travel opportunities, or a museum curator for my knowledge of history.

Perhaps we need a change of scenery. The apartment was fine when I was a bachelor, but we could move into a house. It will stretch credulity that a simple university instructor could afford a house in Vancouver proper, but the important people in my life already know who I am, so there is no need to hide.

In a few years, when Minnie and I don't show signs of aging fast enough to fool her acquaintances, we will move to a new town. That will relieve my boredom.

I wish she weren't out. Whenever Minnie leaves, she takes a piece of me with her.

A loud thump in the hallway ignites my curiosity, and I peek my head out the door.

Mrs. Watson, my neighbor and the wife of my deceased friend and chess partner Gary Watson, struggles with a large suitcase across her threshold. I spring forward to help.

"Oh! Merry, you startled me," she says with a hand on her heart. "I couldn't hear you over the racket of this blasted suitcase."

"Please, let me take it for you." I grab the handle of the plastic-sided case and heave it up. Mrs. Watson sighs in gratitude.

"Thank you, my dear."

"Going somewhere?" I ask as I follow her to the elevator.

"Leaving." At my confused look, she elaborates. "I'm moving in with my daughter, Nellie. She lives in Langley. There's no point rattling around this apartment without Gary."

She tries a half-smile, but her strands seize at the mention of her late husband. My stomach shrivels into a withered ball of guilt. Gary died helping me in the battle against Xenia's minions. He didn't have to, and it was his choice, but the fact remains that he wouldn't have died had he not seen me that day.

I can justify all the reasons why I'm not responsible, and they would be true, but that doesn't remove the sinking sensation in my heart.

The elevator pings, and Mrs. Watson leads us inside.

"I wanted to thank you for the dinner rolls," she says. "A few weeks ago. How did you know which ones to get?"

Gary, with his dying breath, asked me to get them. It was his errand that day, and he wanted to make sure his wife was taken care of.

"He must have mentioned it at some point."

Mrs. Watson hums a little ditty under her breath. Her strands squirm as she tries not to cry in front of me. I know the signs.

There is so little I can do for her—nothing will take away the pain of losing her life's companion—but I can help in my own way. My fingers sneak behind her back until they grasp a loose lauvan. I twist it around my index finger and pour my intention into the strand.

Little by little, her squirming strands calm. She takes a deep sigh, and her shoulders relax. My ministrations dulled the grief slightly and will last for a few days. I can't count the times that I wanted to perform that trick on myself, but I can't manipulate my own emotions.

"Gary was a good man," I say into the silence. "I'll miss him very much."

Mrs. Watson blinks rapidly.

"Me too, dear. Me too." She looks me in the eye and smiles briefly. "But it would have come sooner or later. I had plenty of good years with the old bugger. I count myself lucky."

I stroll into my first class, and the students look surprised to see me on time for once. I can't say I blame them. There was a tumultuous stretch of missed classes a few weeks ago when we last battled Xenia and her minions, and my ambition to give the students my full attention has waned of late. My walk from van to classroom was at a hurried pace from the storm raging outside, evident from flickering lights overhead and blasts of air that rattle the windows.

"Good morning," I say to the group. "You've done your readings, of course. Let's discuss the Old English poem The Dream of the Rood." At one young man's confused expression, I point at him sharply. "Azad, what is the rood?"

He looks panicked and casts his eyes around the room. Someone must mouth the answer to him because he looks at me with relief.

"The Christian cross," he says.

"I'm glad to see you have friends," I say. "I would rather you come to class prepared. Start by reading from page forty-five."

Azad recites the passage with precise enunciation and exaggerated emphasis. He must be taking drama electives.

"'It seemed to me that I saw a most rare tree reach high aloft, wound in light, brightest of beams. All that beacon was covered with gold; gems stood fair where it met the ground, five here above about the crosspiece. Many hosts of angels gazed on it, fair in the form created for them.'"

"Good," I say. "Mariyana, tell us your thoughts on why the rood is covered with gems. Why did the poet depict it so?"

Mariyana looks thoughtful.

23

"I guess the gems and gold are an easy way to show the rood's importance and value to the poet. It's an instrument of torture, and made of rough wood nailed together, but it's also hugely significant to Christians. Maybe the poet figured it needed jazzing up to make it more holy, be taken more seriously. All the churches back then were covered in gold and precious things."

"Excellent point. Humans tend to value beauty and magnificence. Describing the rood covered in gold is a simple way to elevate it in the reader's mind. But what of..."

We continue our discussion for the rest of the hour. Once I dismiss the class, I saunter to the departmental office to check my mailbox. The admin assistant smiles at me, which immediately puts me on guard. He doesn't like me, and he wouldn't smile at me unless there were bad news.

"The Dean wants to see you," he says. "I can schedule an appointment right now if you like. How does Monday at noon work? I see your final morning class ends then."

I'll miss lunch with Minnie, a Monday ritual I have enjoyed greatly. Irrationally strong anger flares in my chest, and I tamp it down before I reply.

"That will do fine. Pencil me into the Dean's busy schedule."

Whoops, some snark escaped. I nod at the admin and swiftly retreat.

Why would the Dean want to see me, of all people? I'm a simple instructor—no professorship strivings here and no graduate students to supervise—and pay raises are strictly regulated by the union. What could she possibly have to discuss with me? I'm generally good at flying under the radar, and it bothers me that I have attracted the Dean's attention.

24

Minnie growls from the living room after work.

"Hurry up, Merry. I'm starving out here."

"Good things come to those who wait." I smear another swirl of icing on the cake and nod in satisfaction. It's a simple lemon sponge, but I have frosted it with pale blue swirls that look like ocean waves. A quick dusting of icing sugar on the tips for froth, and it's ready. I grab two forks, whisk the cake up from the counter, and sail into the other room.

Minnie moans with hunger when I enter, then her eyes widen as they absorb the cake.

"It's gorgeous," she breathes. "The ocean in a storm, of course. Your decorating skills haven't rusted over the years."

"It was only a few decades ago that I was a pastry chef," I protest. "Give me some credit. My brain isn't entirely mush."

Minnie smiles with fond memory.

"Remember the cake that looked like a towering cloud? Our neighbors Sharon and Bill couldn't believe it. And then the inside had alternating layers of blue and chocolate cake. I laughed so hard."

I grin in remembrance.

"And the red velvet cake, where I convinced you that you had the date of your birthday wrong—I changed the calendars to show the wrong date, called in sick to work to pretend it was still the weekend—and you screamed when you saw the candles?"

Minnie chuckles and picks up a fork.

"I remember." She holds her fork expectantly. "What's the protocol? Plates, a knife?"

"Dig in." I spear the cake with my fork and bring a chunk of blue and pale yellow to my mouth. Minnie smiles and stabs the cake with relish. She moans when the flavors hit her tongue.

"Amayshing," she mumbles through a mouthful of cake then

swallows. "Like an explosion of sugar and butter in my mouth."

"Then I did something right."

I spear another piece on my fork and chew thoughtfully. Those cakes I made for Josephine's birthdays were glorious creations, but they masked my inner turmoil. I poured my energy into creating masterpieces so that I wouldn't dwell on the reason for making them. With every magnificent cake, Josephine stepped closer to our inevitable parting.

Minnie is now a year older, and the thought pierces my heart. My emotion must show on my face, for Minnie puts her fork down and tilts her head to study me.

"I recognize that expression," she says. "It's the sad birthday face you always used to make."

My eyebrows lift. I didn't realize my inner turmoil had been so obvious. Minnie chuckles at my surprise.

"Of course I noticed, honestly. How unobservant did you think I was? But you don't need to pull it now. Remember, I'm half-elemental too."

Relief floods through me. In the busyness of cake-making, I forgot our previous realization.

"That's true. You should be around for a lot longer now. I don't know how long, but longer than usual, I hope."

"Good thing I'm not part fire elemental." Minnie licks errant blue icing off her finger. "Do you think they burn hot and fast?"

"Todd is still around, and he's part fire elemental," I say with a frown. Todd, another half-elemental that I discovered last month, has an affinity for both fire and air. I hadn't considered Todd's lifespan. Will he live as long as I have, or will his time on Earth be shorter? He is already eighty-one.

"He's also part air elemental. Maybe that helps him. Where is he these days, anyway?"

"He didn't want to have lessons anymore, so I let him be. I think he was frightened by the elemental battle with Xenia's minions, and I can't blame him. I'll give him some space before I reach out again."

"Suits me." Minnie wrinkles her nose. "He creeps me out. Too power-hungry for my liking, not enough ethics. He would have fit right in at Potestas."

"Can you imagine? He would have been their mascot."

"Their god, more like."

Minnie's comment reminds me of Xenia. I try to let the thought go—live and let live, if she's letting others live—but uneasiness plagues me whenever I think of her. Minnie's mind must trace the same path.

"What do you think Xenia is doing?" she says. "It feels weird, her recruitment. Why would she do that?"

"I don't know." I take another bite of cake, but my tongue doesn't taste the flavors while my mind turns over Minnie's question. "Perhaps it's her way of experiencing Earth. That used to be her main goal. She has been cooped up in partial dormancy since her rebirth, and now she's enjoying herself. If she gets her jollies having people bow and scrape to her, I don't see the harm."

"That's pretty callous," Minnie says in a sharp tone. "What about the bowers and scrapers? Don't they have a say?"

"They don't have to follow Xenia, no matter what she preaches. They all have free will. If they're brainless enough to fall for Xenia's tricks, that's their lookout."

"Wow," says Minnie. "So much for social justice. If someone falls through the cracks in your world, do they deserve it?"

"That's not what I said at all," I say in annoyance. Why is she twisting my words?

Minnie puts her hand up to stop me. It's shaking.

27

"Just, stop," she says in a quieter voice. "Can we change the topic? I'm having trouble reining it in."

I nod but don't trust myself to speak. Minnie's snappiness is from her elemental personality, I assume, but it's emerging more frequently with every passing day. It's unnerving, and I wonder where it will end. Will the Minnie I love eventually be lost in the waves of this argumentative, prickly woman who doesn't seem to like me?

CHAPTER IV

Dreaming

Celeste coughs, a deep sound from her frail chest that rattles alarmingly. When the coughing fit is over, she slumps into her pillows, looking drained.

"Some water, *ma cherie*?" I ask.

She shakes her head weakly.

"It won't be long, now," she says hoarsely. "I can feel death coming."

I clutch her hand reflexively as if to pull her from the grip of death itself. She lets out a wheeze that might be laughter.

"I'm not afraid, my love," she says. "It's time. I'm old, and it is the way of things."

"For most," I mutter.

"For most," she agrees and strokes my fingers. "For me. I'm only sorry to leave you behind. My comfort is that after your grief, you will meet another wonderful woman whom you will adore the way you adore me. You have a big heart, Merle. Don't lock it away."

I squeeze her hand again when she closes her eyes, exhausted by her short speech. Locking away my heart sounds like a reasonable solution, if it would prevent the pain that pierces my chest.

I shovel the last scoop of dirt onto Isabella's grave and lean on the tool, panting for breath. It isn't right that I am the only one here at Isabella's funeral, but the fever took so many this year. It swept through eleventh century Spain, targeting the cities. Isabella's brother and both her parents died from it last week, and her sister lives in a nearby village and dares not travel to plague-ridden Toledo, not even for her sister's death. I don't blame her. There was nothing I could do to prevent this sickness, no matter how I twisted Isabella's strands with desperate intent.

The graveyard is full of hastily dug piles of fresh dirt, the headstones little more than wooden crosses. There is no time for anything more, and we are lucky that the Christian graveyard has room and the manpower to dig graves. Across the city, I have heard stories of bodies heaped into stinking piles, awaiting a burial that might never come.

The hard labor distracted me from my thoughts, but now they flood back. Isabella is gone, and only I am left. There is nothing for me here, not without her laughing eyes and cheeky smiles. She was what I stayed for. Now, I will continue my endless, aimless wandering, carrying my grief like a sack of rocks upon my back.

It's a long trek to Khutulun's burial place, far from the bustling camp of her nomadic people. The Mongolian steppes are windy today, with the stiff breeze waving tall grasses like a father rustling the hair of his child. I am alone but for my sturdy horse, for the sun is hardly breaking over the horizon. The family will venture here later, but I have no desire to join them. They do not like or trust me, and I prefer to visit Khutulun's body alone. I don't wish my thoughts to be disturbed by crying, chanting, or whatever expressions of grief they find necessary to perform. For her brothers, it is all a show. They detested Khutulun, and I'm sure they shed no real tears over her passing.

The hill where Khutulun's body lies is straight ahead, and I brace myself for what I will find. The Mongolians practice open-air burials for all except the Khan and a few select male nobles. Khutulun did not qualify so she was laid here, naked but for a cloth over her face, to be sacrificed to predatory animals.

It's the last, truly virtuous act a person can do, for it allows other animals to live longer. How fast the predators eat the body will tell us how pure the person was and how quickly they will return to heaven to be reborn.

The whole thing turns my stomach when I picture Khutulun's beautiful body ravaged by vultures and wild dogs, but I suppose it is no different from worms digging through dead flesh. At least it is quicker.

I reach the top of the rise. It has been three days since we left her here, and I scan the grass for signs of the body.

There are a few ragged scraps and bones, but the scavengers have picked her clean. I exhale in relief. I didn't want to see her partially eaten body.

It's curious how the Mongolians believe in rebirth just as those in my homeland did during my childhood. It strengthens my resolve to wait for Arthur, slim though the chances of his return might be.

And, perhaps, Khutulun might be reborn as well. The thought brings the only cheer to this grief-stricken time. With a click of my tongue to my horse, I canter away from my eighth wife's remains, to the west and a new life.

I wake up, sweating and shaking from the deluge of

emotional dreams. Minnie's soft breathing interrupts my overwrought thoughts, and I turn my head to look at her soft features in the dim light. She is here with me now, and that's all that matters. A smile tugs my mouth as I drift back to sleep.

CHAPTER V

The emotions that wracked my dreams don't fade in the morning light. When it's time to wake up, I shuffle closer to Minnie and wrap my arms around her.

"Good morning," I whisper in her ear.

Minnie snuggles into me for three blissful minutes, then she pats my arm and wriggles to a sitting position. She grabs her phone off her night table and reads a news site.

"We should stay in bed all morning," I say. "Call in sick to work. Play hooky."

"Mm-hmm," she says. "Maybe if I didn't have clients waiting for me. One of them is in the middle of a crisis, so this is an important visit this morning."

"Fine," I say and settle my head in her lap. She strokes my hair absently.

"Have you heard about those typhoons off the coast of the Philippines? The waves are unreal, two ships are swamped already. Wow, half the crew is still missing, presumed dead." She reads more. "Scientists say that storms are expected this time of year, but the wind speeds are unprecedented."

"How strange," I say without really listening. The Philippines feels too far away from this bed. "I lived in Manila for a few months in the eighteen eighties, you know. Tumultuous times, with the rebellions against the Spanish. Delicious food, though. I could use a nice lechon—bamboo spit roasted pig—right now. And followed up by steamed fermented rice cake with coconut milk. Called bibingka, if I remember right. The favors really sang."

Minnie finishes reading her phone and gently shoves my head off her lap. I let it flop to the mattress without ceremony. She chuckles and jumps off the bed in the direction of the shower.

By the time I wander to the kitchen, yawning from my dream-riddled lack of sleep, Minnie is pouring coffee into two mugs and munching a slice of toast. I slide my hands around her waist.

"You're quick this morning." I nuzzle her neck. "What's the rush?"

She disentangles herself from my arms and reaches into the fridge for her lunch.

"Clients, I told you. And I have a meeting this afternoon with Dave Stanton from Coastal Wellness Clinic. He went to a conference last month and learned some new methods. He said he could pass them on to me, so I'm taking him out for coffee."

A hot flush expands in my chest, unexpected and unwelcome.

"Do you know this guy?" I say, aiming to keep my voice even. "You've never mentioned him before."

"I've known of him for years, but I met him at a mixer last Christmas. He's a good guy, really genuine, and always on top of the research. I wish I had gone to that conference, but chatting to Dave is the next best thing."

My lips are tight, and my heart pounds uncomfortably. What the hell is the matter with me? It takes a moment to recognize the sensation as jealousy. The thought startles me so much that the feeling ebbs. Jealous? I have never had reason to be jealous with Minnie before. What has changed now?

Minnie peers at me, trying to gauge my mood. Her eyes narrow.

"Oh, no you don't," she says. "You are not getting possessive. I won't stand for it. I married you, didn't I?" She brandishes her hand at me with the ring gleaming golden on her finger. "Do not mistrust me." She slams her coffee on the counter. "I need space, and I need trust. You being possessive

34

gives me neither and only forces a wedge between us. I suggest you figure this out today because I don't want to see it again."

I look away, anger and shame keeping me silent. I don't understand why I mistrust her now when I never have in the past. What is different? The memory of Minnie's sharp tones rings through my head. It's not Minnie I don't trust, it's this new personality that is emerging. I don't know it at all. Minnie is someone I have known for centuries. This new person is a wild card.

Will the new personality take over one day? The thought terrifies me. What would that mean for the future? Would Minnie leave me entirely, to be replaced by a cold stranger? Would her personality change enough that she wouldn't want me anymore?

It won't help to tell Minnie this now. She's already on edge and is trying her hardest to keep a damper on her other side. I pick up my mug of coffee and take a gulp of the scalding liquid. It burns going down, but the discomfort distracts me from the pain of our confrontation.

Minnie takes a deep breath and speaks in a calmer tone.

"Did you look at the material I left you?"

I answer, happy to latch onto a new topic.

"I glanced at the book. The personality test verged on the absurd and didn't tell me much that I don't already know. It didn't seem that helpful."

"You could try volunteering somewhere," Minnie says. "Many people find purpose in helping others. Selfless acts are also fulfilling. It might give you ideas to pursue."

I shrug. I have tried most things in this world. I doubt slopping soup into a bowl will tell me much about myself.

"I'll probably put career ideas in a hat and pick one out at random."

Minnie sighs sharply, her attempt at restraint clearly over.

"You can be dissolute about your own career, but I am committed to mine. I'll see you after work. Don't check up on me."

She gives me a perfunctory kiss on the cheek and strides to the hallway. The front door closes a moment later.

I scrub my face and sigh. Every interaction with Minnie these days feels like a minefield. One false move, and everything blows up in my face.

I pull out a chair and slump into it. The pages of my personality test waver in the breeze of my movement, and I pick up a page. Perhaps I should go through these again, do another test. I don't want to lose Minnie because she thinks I'm aimless or without ambition. It feels like a sticking point with her these days.

I fill out another test, and there is a list of possible career options. I run my fingers down the list. Paramedic, soldier, professional athlete, actor. I have been a doctor, soldiering was my life for centuries, sports lack the life-or-death thrill of battle, and acting is too high-profile. Nothing speaks to me, and nothing promises to fill the void of dissatisfaction. I push the papers aside and stand. I need a distraction.

Jen clips on her harness the next day.

"I'm glad you came with me, Merry," she says. "We haven't hung out properly for ages."

"It has been a while," I agree. "Your love life is terribly unwieldy."

Jen snorts and whacks my arm with the back of her hand.

"Let's not talk about it. I am over men. I'm doing things for me right now."

36

"Over men forever?"

Jen giggles.

"Maybe not forever. But for now. There was way too much drama. Part of it was me, I'll take my share of the blame. But part of it was this past lives grail nonsense, which is enough to turn anyone's head into a swirling pile of goo."

"So poetic," I murmur. Jen swats me again.

"It's true. I feel much better about being me and this huge line of other women, but I want some time to really get comfortable in my own skin again before I introduce new complications."

"Relationships can be complicated," I say.

Jen narrows her eyes at me.

"Is everything okay with you and Minnie?"

"Everything's fine," I say shortly. I don't want to get into our drama right now. I want to forget about it and distract myself from the oddness at home. If I think about Minnie's changes too much, a molten feeling of unidentifiable dread threatens to fill my abdomen.

Jen doesn't press, although her golden lauvan tell me that she knows something is up.

"That harness is really styling," she says instead. "I love the bunching effect with your clothes."

I pose to elicit a laugh, then we walk along a woodchip path to a sturdy conifer tree with a ladder. Far up the tree is a platform and a cable that spans to a distant tree through the forest. A shriek of terror and delight filters through the canopy.

"What prompted ziplining?" I ask when we reach the ladder.

"I haven't done it before. I'm trying new things to expand my horizons and test my boundaries. I'm not great with heights, not since my accident." An enemy shoved Jen off a cliff a few months ago, and she would have been paralyzed had I not healed her with my abilities. "I figured ziplining was a safe way to push myself."

"And have some fun, too."

"And that. I'm really enjoying getting out without reference to anyone else. It's fun hanging out with me." Her strands wiggle with the slight untruth. She misses having a boyfriend, but she is enjoying her alone time as well. People are complicated creatures.

"And me."

"And you."

She smiles, but I point to the ladder.

"Ladies first. Let's test these boundaries of yours."

Jen takes a deep breath then places her hands on the ladder and heaves herself up. I give her a few rungs' head start then follow.

The platform is dizzyingly high, and tree roots below are nothing but twigs. Jen grips the railing with whitened knuckles.

"Let's strap you in." I help her trembling fingers clip her carabiner to the cable. "There. Now you won't fall."

"So you say." Jen tugs at the strap holding her to the cable. "My mind knows it's sturdy, but my heart is telling me to get down now."

"I've never taken you flying, have I?"

Jen shakes her head with vigor.

"I've never asked you to, for good reason. Ziplining is hard enough."

"Do this, then consider it." I look to the sky where a crow circles lazily overhead. "There's nothing quite like it. And the avian instincts would take away your fears, I guarantee it."

Jen gives me a tight smile then turns to the gap in the railing. She gulps audibly.

"You know what, Merry?" She glances back at me with wide eyes. "You're going to have to push me for this first one."

"Truly?"

She nods, and only then do I allow an evil grin to spread across my face. Her mouth opens.

"Wait, I changed—"

Before she can finish her sentence, I grasp her waist and heave her over the edge. Her shrieks pierce my ears, and curses drift back to me.

"That's not very ladylike, Jen," I call out. When she reaches the far side and collapses on the deck, I strap myself in and leap off the edge.

Wind whistles past my ears and makes my eyes water. It's hard to think about my issues with Minnie with the exhilaration of motion. I'm glad I came out with Jen today.

An hour later, we arrive breathless and red-cheeked at my van in the parking lot. Jen's black hair blows free of her braid and twines with her golden lauvan. She is bright-eyed and joyful, and her cheer rubs off on me as it always used to do. It's one of the reasons I like being around her.

"That was great," Jen says when she hops into the passenger's seat. "Too much fun."

"No such thing. Next time, we'll use feathers?"

Jen bites her lip, but there is a gleam of adventure in her eyes.

"I guess so."

"Deal."

My phone rings, and I glance at the screen.

"Why is Cecil calling me?" I murmur. Jen's ex-boyfriend, although a member of our group of friends, is not in the habit of phoning. Jen looks at me sharply. I answer the phone. "Hi,

Cecil."

"Hi, Merry. Sorry to disturb you, but I need to ask you something." Cecil's voice is hesitant. Jen leans closer to me to eavesdrop, so I increase the volume of the phone.

"Ask away."

"You wiped the memories of the Potestas members in the sacrifice cave, right? Anna Green was one of them, but she seems fine now. Are there any side effects to wiping memories?"

I frown. Why is he asking this?

"Yes, there can be," I say slowly. "Some of those people turned to vegetables, remember? Anna was one of the lucky ones. I had terrible conditions to work in, though. I also didn't particularly care about the outcome. They had all just tried to kill Minnie, so I wasn't in a charitable mood. If I take my time, my rate of success is much higher."

There is silence on the line. I hate phones for that. There are no lauvan to gauge reactions by. Jen and I share a glance.

"Why do you ask?" I say.

"Oh, just wondering." Cecil sounds thoughtful. "Sorry to bug you. Thanks. Bye."

He hangs up, and I'm left staring at my phone. I place it on the console and look at Jen.

"What was that about?"

"Why would he want to know how safe memory wiping is, unless he wants to do it on someone?" Jen says. I tap my fingers on the steering wheel.

"Does he have someone in his life that he would want that for? An abusive family member, perhaps, or someone he's wronged that he wants forgiveness from?"

Jen shakes her head.

"Not that I know about. I wonder." An arrested look chases over Jen's face. "Does he want to use it on himself?"

40

Understanding floods me.

"He doesn't want to remember his past lives."

"I get that, I really do." Jen sighs and stares out the windshield. "I would have considered that early on, honestly." She bites her lip and turns to me. Her strands wave uncertainly. "Do you think it has anything to do with me? Is it my fault?"

I shrug.

"He's a grown man and can make his own decisions. Don't blame yourself for other people's actions. By all means, call him and see if he'll tell you what he's thinking, but don't place the burden on your own shoulders."

"I guess." She sags into the seat. "So messy. This is why I'm on my own right now."

My mind drifts to Minnie and her hard face when she left. I turn on the car.

"Messy, indeed."

We are silent while I pull into traffic. Jen taps her fingers on her knee but keeps her thoughts to herself.

"Do you ever wonder if Gary was someone we knew?" I say. Cecil's desire to erase his past lives has me pondering the rest of my friends. "I never told him about our history, but right before he died, he said he wouldn't want to know even if he had lived before."

"Oh." Jen leans her head against the headrest. "I hadn't thought of that. Wow. Who could he have been? Who isn't accounted for, from the early days?"

"Many. I have no idea how this works. How were you all given multiple rebirths? Was it a slice of time, or an event, or was it something to do with me?"

"I'd bet anything it was you, and I say that despite the ego boost it will give you." Jen smiles when I snort. "No, you're the odd one out, here. It makes sense that it was you. I hope we figure it out one day. But, back to Gary." Her eyes light up, and she chuckles with incredulity. "No. Do you think he was Gareth?"

"Come on, that's too obvious. Just because the names are the same?" I shake my head but compare the two men. The longer I think about it, the more similarities I find. Their open-hearted simplicity, their love of talking and jokes, and their simple loyalty all lend credulity to Jen's theory.

"I'm totally right," Jen declares.

I recall the bowed shoulders of Mrs. Watson in the hall as she left her home.

"I guess we'll never know."

I leave Jen at her apartment and stop at a deli to buy a sandwich. On the way out, as I lick my finger clean of escaping mustard, a familiar poster catches my eye. It's Xenia again, but with a new date for a showing of "miracles and signs" of the presence of an Aztec goddess on Earth.

The sight makes my stomach turn. This goddess complex of Xenia's doesn't feel right. I have ignored it until now, but I need to see for myself what she has planned. Something is not adding up with her antics.

When I get home, Minnie is reading a book on the couch. I'm not sure how to greet her given our confrontation yesterday. The evening was strained, and Minnie left in the morning to see friends. My shoulders relax when she looks up from her book with a smile and pats the couch.

"Hi, love. Where have you been?"

"Ziplining with Jen." I sit and lean into the cushions. Minnie nestles against me, and everything feels right with the world. "She's expanding her horizons and needed someone to go with

42

since she's sworn off dating for the near future."

Minnie chuckles.

"We'll see how long that lasts. But good for her."

I rub her arm and we sit in comfortable silence for a moment until Xenia's poster swims in my mind's eye.

"I think I need to see Xenia in person," I say into the quiet. Minnie stiffens beside me. "I don't know what her game is, and it's bothering me."

Minnie sits up.

"I was hoping you'd say that. I agree. She's acting fishy. Just because she can't summon more minions from the elemental plane doesn't mean she can't make mischief here. But this should be a stealth mission. I don't want her to recognize us."

"Disguises are easy." I grin. "How about I do you and you do me? You can decide how you want me to look for the day."

Minnie laughs.

"You might regret this."

CHAPTER VI

Xenia's meeting, or worship gathering, or whatever moniker makes sense for a showing of miracles, is happening Sunday at noon, so I call Alejandro the next day before we leave to see if he wants to come. There's no answer.

"We'll stop by his place," Minnie says. She adjusts her shirt. "It's on the way. I want to show him my handiwork."

I stroke my handlebar mustache.

"You don't think the facial hair stands out too much?"

"Not as much as these ridiculous jugs," Minnie says. She tugs her shirt again. "Seriously, I'm getting a backache."

"I only gave you them because of the pipes you landed me with." I flex my muscles. "I didn't realize Hulk Hogan was your secret fantasy."

Minnie giggles and presses her chest to mine.

"Fun for a day, anyway. Maybe later I'll test drive your new bod."

"Or we could try them out now." I run my hands up her sides in a direct path to her newly enhanced chest. She laughs, kisses me firmly under my moustache, then pushes me away.

"Come on, let's show Alejandro. We'll let him decide what he wants, though. The poor guy can't get back at us if we're too mean."

I knock on the door of Alejandro and Liam's basement suite with a meaty fist. There's movement in the side window, then the door opens. Liam blinks at us.

"Yes?"

"I heard you're part of fight club," I growl. "Show me what you've got."

Liam's eyes widen, but to his credit, he doesn't flinch. Instead, his spine straightens.

Minnie can't keep her face straight and bursts out in laughter.

"Calm down, Liam. It's Minnie and Merry."

Liam blinks again, then his expression eases and he grins.

"That's wild." He scans us up and down. I step forward.

"Stop checking out my woman," I say in a threatening tone then chuckle. "This voice is great. I could get used to it."

"Why don't you change looks more often?" Liam steps back to let us in. "What a talent."

"What are you saying, you prefer the handlebars?" I smooth my mustache. "It's too much work to hold for long. I do it if I need to, but it's a strain."

I stride inside and run my hand over the huge round table in Liam's kitchen. Alejandro couldn't resist buying it, and I have grown rather fond of it myself. It hearkens back to our earliest days when Arthur tried to keep the peace among fractious allies.

"Where's Alejandro?" I say. "We're going to check out Xenia's prayer team today and thought he'd want to come. You're welcome too, of course."

"He's in his room, getting ready for a date," Liam says. "Lots of those lately."

"Anyone sticking?"

Alejandro decided a few weeks ago to stop holding a candle for Jen and move on with his life. He's been so busy that I have scarcely seen him, but I don't begrudge him the time. I'm pleased he's not moping for Jen anymore. I still hold hope that they might find each other once more, but sighing longingly wasn't a winning strategy.

"Not that I've heard." Liam shrugs. "He holds his cards tight to his chest."

I bend to look under the table. The grail is housed there, dangling in a cloth bag from a hook I installed weeks ago. It seemed like a good place to keep the grail where everyone could access it. It isn't mine, after all, and the decision to touch it should be in the hands of those who want to see their past lives, not me.

The hook is empty.

I whirl around and stare at Liam.

"Where is the grail?" I force out. My chest, massive in this form, is still too constrictive for the burning fear building inside. Liam frowns and looks under the table.

"I don't know." He takes a closer look at me. "Whoa, chill, Merry. I'm sure it's somewhere."

"It's an important artifact," I grind out. My fist mashes in my other palm. "We can't misplace it. It's too important to us. It needs to stay where we can all find it."

Minnie puts a hand my shoulder, but even her touch fails to calm me. A part of me understands that my wild anger is irrational, but I can't control it. The loss of the grail hits me like a punch to the face.

"The grail can't be treated like an old sock. When I placed it here, I expected it to be taken care of."

The door to Alejandro's room swings open. Alejandro, his thick black hair unusually tamed, stops when he sees us with a look of surprise until Liam speaks.

"Don't worry, it's Merry and Minnie. Do you know where the grail went?"

Alejandro shakes his head at the revelation of our identities but focuses on the question.

"I was cleaning it. It should be behind the dish rack."

I stride to the sink. Sure enough, on a carefully folded towel

46

behind a rack of plates is the grail. Its aquamarine and rusty red enamel is a familiar sight. I grasp its stemless bowl with a sigh of relief.

"Good. I'll put it back where it belongs."

I spend longer under the table than is strictly necessary to hang a cup. My heart still races, and I try to calm myself. Why did I react so strongly to the missing grail?

It's the reason I know Minnie and my friends are who they are. Without it, I would still be lost and alone. The thought of a future without the grail, once the others have died, shakes me to my very center. I can't endure another fifteen centuries without them.

The future is too uncertain and too difficult to contemplate, so I climb out from under the table to rejoin the conversation.

"Love the disguises," Alejandro says. "I'm sorry I can't come with you. I'm meeting Amelia for drinks."

"Have you dated her before?" Minnie asks.

"No, she's new." Alejandro sighs. "I'm not used to this dating game. It's interesting, though, meeting new people. I like that part."

"Keep trying." Minnie squeezes his elbow. "The right woman is out there for you."

"I need to pick up my niece this afternoon," Liam says. "She's staying for a week while my sister is away for work. But if you don't mind dropping me off at the bus station after, I can come along for reinforcements."

"I'm hoping there won't be a battle where we need reinforcements," I say. "But company is always welcome. Now, do you have any requests for your disguise?"

Minnie glances at Liam with a critical eye.

"I think you suit green eyes," she says.

"Fun for a change, anyway," Liam says. "Whoa, what's going on here?"

We all stop short. Where there were once three magnificent houses perched on a steep hillside between the road and the water's edge, a massive hole now gapes in the dirt and rock. Two yellow excavators dig relentlessly into the slope. The construction site is filled with people, more than is necessary for the work being done. Everyone has a shovel or tool of some kind and works industriously. I glance at the others.

"Those houses weren't old," I say. "Who bought all three and then tore them down?"

"And what are they building?" Liam asks.

"It's Xenia," Minnie says. "She's in March's body, with March's memories and access to her funds. She bought the site, but why?"

I point at a group of people that cluster near the ocean on the only flat spot.

"Our answers might be there. Come on, let's meet Coatlicue's daughter."

We pick our way down a makeshift driveway of gravel along the edge of the property, tracing the neighbor's cedar fence as we go. The site is dazzling with glittering ocean as the backdrop. A large lauvan earth cable slides through the middle of the property and descends into the sea at the bottom.

The meeting place is not as flat as it appeared from the road, and we carefully join the crowd while watching for loose rocks. I glance casually at our fellow worshipers. Some have clearly misplaced their tinfoil hats and mutter to themselves. Some have crossed arms that advertise them as skeptics here for a show to heckle. Some look curious, possibly passersby who were wondering what the fuss was about.

A few interspersed among the crowd have an aura of fervor. I overhear one speak to his neighbor.

"She's the real deal. You've never seen anything like it."

This must not be the first time Xenia has displayed her miracles. I wonder what's in store for us today.

A babble of chatter breaks out, and then a hush falls over the crowd. I look around until a figure climbs into view on a platform that I hadn't noticed until now.

It's Xenia. She has dressed March's body in a flowing blouse and long skirt better suited to an anthropology textbook than Vancouver waterfront, in shades of sandy brown with shells embroidered along the edge of the skirt. A mossy green belt is tied in a sweeping fashion around her waist, and a diadem of branches adorns her forehead. March's hair was once cut in a stylish bob, but now flows loosely around her ears. She has an earthy, wholesome look, but with a regal bearing. She must have worked hard to come up with the right outfit.

Her piercing eyes, lacking none of March's intensity despite Xenia looking through them, scan the crowd. I'm thankful for our disguises. Although she knows my lauvan are brown, my half-elemental status isn't evident without closer inspection, and many other humans share the color of my strands.

She raises her hands in benediction, and the quiet crowd silences. Even the skeptics and passersby want to hear the words of this madwoman whose bearing is anything but.

"The earth feels your presence," she calls out. "Your essences are connected to the greater whole. You may think yourselves separate from Mother Earth, but she is with you, everywhere. I, too, was once where you are now. I was unenlightened, feeling myself apart from creation." She lowers her voice a fraction, and I find myself leaning forward with the rest to catch her words. "Coatlicue came to me. The ground

49

shook under my feet, and great rocks fell from the heights. I was petrified and fell to my knees, thinking that the end was near.

"And it was." Xenia stares around for effect. "My life as I knew it was over. Coatlicue said to me, 'You are my daughter, born of mortal woman. You had a mortal name but that is not who you are. I now name you Xenia, daughter of Coatlicue, and your powers will be legendary. All who see you will be amazed. Build me a house of worship, and you and your followers will never want again.'"

There is a moment of silence, then a man at the back shouts.

"Where's our wine, Jesus?"

There are a few guffaws at the heckle. Xenia smiles impassively then puts out her hands. Only Minnie and I see the strands between her fingers.

I stumble as the ground trembles underfoot. A few people scream in shock, then babbling breaks out.

"She is Xenia, daughter of Coatlicue!" The man whom I overheard speaking to his neighbor about Xenia before yells out. "Follow her, and you shall never go wanting!"

More hecklers shout about coincidences, and expressions of shock and fear chase over many faces. I glance at Minnie and Liam, who stare back at me with confusion. Why is Xenia doing this? It's an uphill battle to convert others to a religion, even if she can make the earth shake.

The crowd gets louder and more boisterous. Fear for our safety drives me toward the back of the group. Liam and Minnie stay close to me.

Xenia looks calm and collected as chaos erupts around her. She raises her hands, and I brace myself for another tremor. Instead, strands around the heads of those nearest to her writhe and twist into a new conformation. The twisting spreads from person to person, and it leaves behind calm and quiet.

50

I don't know what's happening, but I don't like it. I push Minnie in front of me to escape whatever Xenia is doing, with Liam on my heels. I don't look back until we are five paces away from the outermost person.

Liam faces us, but a look of dreamy unconcern washes over his face. The expression is mirrored on the faces of everyone in the crowd, which is now quiet. They all turn to Xenia, Liam included, and she smiles at them with beneficent serenity.

"My friends, welcome to the reign of Xenia. Work hard and you shall be rewarded by being allowed to worship me. Fail me, and you will not be seen again."

"We will not fail you," they say in unison, and the hairs on my neck stand up at the toneless chant.

I glance at Minnie, worried about seeing the same complacence on her face, but she looks at me with fear and squeezes my hand. I squeeze her back, relieved beyond measure that she wasn't taken from me.

"We need to get Liam," she whispers. "But Xenia can't notice that we aren't following the script."

I nod and face Xenia, schooling my expression into a mirror of Liam's. Xenia raises her hand and calls out some benediction, but I scarcely hear it through the blood pounding in my ears. Just when I thought Xenia was benign, she proves again how dangerous she truly is. She is controlling the minds of everyone she can lure to her meetings and creating an army that will do her bidding. What that is, I still don't know, but the threat to their safety was clear should they not follow her orders.

And now, Liam is under her spell, and no one is safe from Xenia's machinations. All I want is a world where I can live with Minnie in peace, and Xenia constantly gets in the way of that goal. As much as I wanted to sweep her actions under the rug, I can't let her get away with this. Liam is captured, and anyone could be next. I shiver with fear and rage at the thought of Minnie, her face wiped of lively expression. That can't happen.

Xenia must be stopped, and once again, it's up to me to stop her.

CHAPTER VII

After Xenia dismisses her new followers, they turn and shamble toward the path we are on. For a moment, I worry that they are sent after us, the ones who didn't comply, but their eyes don't look our way. I grab Liam's elbow and steer him to the front of the crowd. Minnie hurries ahead to the van and has the back door open and waiting for me to shove Liam inside. He doesn't resist. His expression is calm and dreamy.

I jump in after him and toss the keys to Minnie.

"Start driving. I'll work on Liam."

Minnie nods and peels out of our parking spot. I push Liam over to make room for me, and he shuffles obligingly. He doesn't defy me, but neither does he initiate movement. His eyes hold none of their usual bright inquisitiveness.

I focus on the snarl of lauvan at his temple. It's a tiny knot but wound so tightly that I can only unpick the top few threads. When I sit back to gauge the effect of my work, Liam gazes back with a blank stare.

"Anything?" Minnie says from the front seat.

"The knot is so tight I can hardly budge it. Perhaps you can get your fingernails in later."

"I'll try." Minnie takes a hard left, away from Liam's house.

"Where are you going?"

"We still have to pick up Liam's niece, remember?"

I had completely forgotten Liam's errand in the turmoil of our narrow escape. My eyes rake over Liam's placid face.

"How are we going to explain Uncle Liam's state?"

At a red light, Minnie glances back at us, her forehead creased.

"I'll try untangling in the parking lot. But if you can't do it, I doubt I'll be able to loosen the knot. We'll just have to say he isn't feeling well. Speaking of which, I was hoping you could drop me off at Inna's house afterward. I told her I'd help her this afternoon. She just got out of surgery."

"What am I supposed to do with this?" I indicate Liam. Minnie shrugs.

"I'm afraid we'll have to stop Xenia first. As soon as I get home, we'll figure out how to take that bitch down."

Minnie turns around with her jaw set. I look at Liam again.

"Can you hear me, Liam?" I say quietly. "Say something."

"What would you like me to say?" he says clearly. My heart leaps. Perhaps he isn't as far gone as I feared.

"How are you feeling?"

"Great, thanks."

"What do you think about Xenia?"

Liam's face lights up. It's the first passionate expression I have seen since he was mindwiped.

"Xenia, daughter of Coatlicue, performer of miracles. She is worthy to be worshiped."

If I needed confirmation of who brainwashed him, I now have it.

"We're picking up your niece now. What's her name?"

"Chloe."

"Good. Now, can you act normally around her?"

Liam looks at me with a blank expression.

"What do you mean?"

I sigh and pat his arm.

"Never mind. I'll do the talking."

Liam's state is worse than I feared. He blindly, fervently believes Xenia is the daughter of this mythical goddess and will aid her in whatever way she wishes. I wonder how far her reach is. Can she command him from afar, or does he need to be close to her?

I feel sick at Liam's state, and how close Minnie was to falling prey to the same doom. My skin crawls at the thought of Minnie smiling with the same manic glee that Liam displayed at the mention of Xenia. I don't know whether it was our half-elemental status that allowed us to escape Liam's fate, or that we were simply far enough away to avoid Xenia's tendrils.

I try to further unknot Liam's strands while Minnie drives, but it's a half-hearted attempt. They are bound too tightly to budge. The van stops at a red light, and with a start I recognize the stretch of road where we battled Xenia's minions a few weeks ago. Half of the awnings are still missing from businesses, and burned buildings beside the blasted construction site are cordoned off with temporary fencing. Everything comes back to Xenia, and the destruction fuels my anger toward the wayward fundamental.

"We're here," Minnie says when she enters the bus station parking lot. She pulls into a vacant spot, kills the engine, and wriggles into the back with us. "Here, let me try."

I point wordlessly at the knot on Liam's temple. Minnie frowns in concentration while she picks at the strands. Liam hums tunelessly and stares straight ahead.

"No dice," Minnie says finally. "I can't loosen them. We need to get Chloe."

"We'll have to bring him along." I poke Liam in the chest, but there's no reaction. "She needs to recognize her uncle."

Minnie looks dubiously at Liam, but she slides open the back door and climbs out. I pull Liam's sleeve and he follows me with wooden motions. We enter the bus station, and I scan the arrival screen for information.

"The bus from Merritt just arrived at platform six," I say. "Come on."

A girl of perhaps fourteen years with braided brown hair and a purple backpack leans against one of the marble pillars that holds up the grand old building. A violin case covered with stickers sits on the floor beside her. Her face lights up when she spies Liam.

"Uncle Liam!" She grabs her violin case and runs toward him. When she throws her arms around him, he's almost bowled over by the motion. He doesn't react to her embrace, so Minnie and I surreptitiously move his arms to hug the girl.

"Hi, Chloe," Minnie says warmly when Chloe steps back. "I'm Minnie and this is Merry. We're friends of Liam's."

"We're the ride," I say. "Is this everything? We're through these doors here."

"Did you have a good trip?" Minnie says. "How long is the drive from Merritt? I'm from the prairies, originally, so I haven't explored much locally yet."

I prod Liam in the back to get him moving, and Minnie and I chatter to Chloe to distract her from Liam's odd behavior. Chloe answers amiably enough, but she casts suspicious glances at Liam's placid face.

"I'm starving," Chloe announces. "I hope you went shopping this time, Uncle Liam. Remember last time, when all there was in your fridge was an old potato and beer? Mum was so pissed when she heard."

Liam merely looks blank with a vacant smile on his face. I prod his side.

"That sounds like you, doesn't it?" I say to him pointedly. Liam finally nods.

"Yeah, it does."

"I'm sure there'll be food," Minnie says. "If not, the grocery store is very close."

56

"Good."

We get to the van and I open the passenger's door for Chloe. Normally, I would make her sit in the back with her uncle, but the pretense of chivalry will give Liam another few minutes without scrutiny. It will happen soon, but I would rather be at Liam's home first.

Chloe swings her violin case in the van and climbs in after it. When Minnie and Liam are settled in the back, I turn the wheels westward. Chloe drums her fingers on her case.

"I hope I'll have lots of time to practice this week," she says with a hint of adolescent petulance. "My grade five exam is coming up. It was such bad timing for Mum to be away this week. Now I can't have my lessons."

"You can practice on your own for a week, surely," I say. My attention is on my driving and Liam's predicament, and I'm only half-following our conversation.

"But what if my teacher can spot the little things that the examiners will look for? Sometimes I think my playing is perfect, but then she finds things that I wouldn't have thought about." Anxiety colors her voice, and I frown.

"If it sounds good to you, why are you worried? Play to please your own ears."

"But I want to pass my exam," she says with exaggerated patience.

I try hard not to glance at Minnie. It has been many years since I have dealt with an adolescent, and I forgot how their antics rankle.

"If I don't pass my exam," she continues. "How can I keep playing?"

My eyebrows raise at this.

"What would stop you?"

I glance at Chloe, who looks puzzled at my question. I sigh and turn back to the windshield.

"If it matters that much to you, I can give you a lesson this week." I will probably be around often if Liam persists in his brainwashed state.

"He's very good," Minnie pipes up from the back, and I smile at her in the rearview mirror.

"Really?" Chloe looks dubious but then nods as she thinks about my offer. "That would be awesome. Thanks. I'll take you up on that."

I drop Minnie off at her friend's house, and we exchange expressive looks before she says goodbye to Chloe and walks down the pavement. A few minutes later, we pull into a free parking spot in front of Liam's place.

"Here we are," I say and turn off the van. "Your new abode for a week."

Chloe looks the house and street over with a critical eye.

"Still a bit grungy, but way nicer than the last place, Uncle Liam."

I need to try untangling Liam's strands again. Surely, with a bit of light and some time, I can persevere.

"Come on in," I say. "Liam, let's show your niece the place."

Liam obligingly opens the door, climbs out of the van, and walks stiffly down the sidewalk. I swiftly follow to cover his strange movements. Chloe trots after us and looks around the neighborhood, her attention off Liam.

Alejandro must have noticed us through the window, for he opens the door as we approach.

"You're back from your date early," I say in surprise. "Didn't it go well?"

"She was okay, but we didn't click, so I ended it early before it got too awkward." Alejandro shrugs. His forest green lauvan droop in despondency, but the ends rise with hope. "Next time, right?"

I pat him on the shoulder.

"Absolutely. Plenty of fish in the sea." I gesture to Chloe, who hovers near my elbow. "Alejandro, meet Liam's niece Chloe. Chloe, meet Liam's roommate Alejandro."

"Nice to meet you." Alejandro holds out his hand with his usual frank eagerness. Chloe grasps it after a moment's hesitation, as if adults don't often extend their hands to her. They likely don't these days, even though Chloe is old enough to be considered an adult in many eras I have lived through.

"Alejandro." I interrupt their greeting. "There was a slight issue at the meeting." I jerk my head toward Liam and gaze at Alejandro expressively. His eyes flick between us, and a frown creases his brow. "Can you show Chloe where she'll sleep and make her some food? I need to speak with Liam."

"Of course." Alejandro may not fully understand what's going on, but he trusts me enough to follow my lead. "Come in, Chloe. What do you like to eat?"

I close the door gently behind them and sit Liam on the stone ledge that follows the walk.

"Hold still, Liam," I mutter. "We're going to fix you."

He smiles blandly and doesn't answer. I shake my head and bring my fingers to the ugly knot in his dusky maroon strands.

Fifteen minutes later, I admit defeat. The knot is impenetrable. Even through my fear and frustration, I admire Xenia's work. How did she manage it? And could I replicate it? A tight manipulation like that would never come undone. Through my prodding and poking, I think I see how it could be achieved and I itch to try it out, but this is no time for experimentation.

I enter the suite with Liam in tow. The remains of a sandwich lie on the round table, and violin music drifts through the crack under Liam's bedroom door. Alejandro stands and hurries to us.

"What happened?" he says in a low voice. "What's wrong

with Liam?"

"Xenia happened," I say and sit heavily in a chair. The others follow my lead, although Liam's movements are stiff and his eyes vacant. I gaze at him for a long moment. "Xenia is manipulating the minds of her followers during these 'miracle' sessions, making them completely subservient to her. When I figured out what she was doing, we ran but Liam got caught. Here, watch." I turn to Liam. "Who is Xenia?"

"Xenia is the daughter of Coatlicue and is my lady to command me."

This pronouncement is said with a passion that lights his face before he reverts to his vacant gaze. Alejandro's eyes are as round as coins.

"She really did a number on him," he breathes. "And you can't fix it?"

"The knot is impenetrable. Impressively so. But now he's in a semi-catatonic state. What do we tell his work, his niece?"

"I can call in sick for him at work," Alejandro says firmly, then he glances at the closed bedroom door. "As for Chloe, I don't know. We'll have to tell her some version of the truth."

I snort.

"That her uncle has been magically mindwiped by an evil spirit? Come on."

"Not that, obviously." Alejandro shakes his head at me. "But something. Maybe that he's not feeling well and is on some medication."

I sigh with relief.

"Brilliant. That will do nicely. And keep an eye on him as much as you can, all right? I'll stop by often until we figure this out."

My phone pings, and I pull it out to see who texted me. It's Cecil, wondering where I am. Why would he want to know?

"We have to stop Xenia," Alejandro says. I quickly dash an

answer to Cecil and put my phone away.

"Yes, we do. Again."

"We'll do it." Alejandro's look of fierce determination makes me smile, and he frowns at me. "What are you grinning at?"

"You reminded me of Arthur for a moment. You really haven't changed, you know."

Alejandro grins before his face settles into a serious expression.

"There are a few angles we can take. First, we need to alert the others." He pulls out his phone and dashes off a text to our group of friends. "There. They need to be on the lookout for Xenia. No one can approach her unless they are prepared. Second, we can slow her down. Don't people need permits or something to do big projects?"

"Yes, that's brilliant. Did Xenia apply for a zoning application? I bet not. I wonder why the site isn't crawling with inspectors and red tape? I'll make some calls, see if we can't drown her project in bureaucracy."

"Good." Alejandro nods with approval. "For our third angle, we need to find protection of some kind."

He races to his room and returns with a binder. When he drops it on the table and flips it open, I recognize the pages.

"Did you photocopy your grandfather's notebook?"

Alejandro's grandfather Braulio was my best friend. When he died, he left me a notebook filled with his years of research into the spirit world. It has come in handy more times than I would care to admit if Braulio and his huge ego were still alive to gloat. I put it with the other books in a vacant apartment I rented for Potestas' elemental library.

"Yes," Alejandro says. "I want to look in it often, so it helps to have my own copy. It doesn't have everything, though, so our fourth step is to look through the spirit library for

61

protection ideas. Fifth, think about how Xenia did the brainwashing. Do you have any idea how she did that? If we know how, maybe we can stop or reverse it."

I gaze at Alejandro as he pours over Braulio's pages. He jumped straight into the problem with no regard to how it will affect him or with any hesitation at all. It's typical Alejandro, typical Arthur. Indeed, it is characteristic of all his past lives. I recall Arnost, who founded an orphanage for children of plague victims. He saw a cause and jumped in with both feet. Alejandro through the ages is always a better man than I am, and I wonder what it would take to emulate him.

"I cut a library key for you, didn't I? I hope this doesn't get in the way of your dating life." I say this in jest, but Alejandro frowns without looking up.

"I'd love to find someone, but making sure others are safe and can live in freedom is far more important."

"Even if Jen pursued you?"

Alejandro looks up with a thoughtful expression.

"Some things are more important than me and my happiness. Whoever I was with would have to understand that."

He returns to the notebook. I stare at his black hair. We are very different men. I admire his pursuits of lofty goals—in every life, whether he found the reborn Guinevere or not, he found ways to help others—but I don't share it. Minnie is paramount to me now that I have found her again.

A knock startles me.

"I'll get the door," I say.

Alejandro nods without looking up, and Liam smiles vacantly. My head shakes as I walk toward the door. We need to find something to break Xenia's hold on Liam.

Cecil shifts from foot to foot outside. His face opens with relief when he sees me.

"Merry, hi," he says. "Can we talk for a minute? Outside?"

"All right." I close the door and stare at him. "What's the matter?"

"I don't want to remember my past," he says in a rush. "It's too much. It's unnecessary. It hasn't brought me anything. I want to go back to the way I was before. Please, Merry, fix my head so I don't remember."

CHAPTER VIII

He gazes at me with pleading eyes, and my lips tighten. Jen was right. He doesn't want to remember.

"Are you certain?" I say finally. "This isn't a reaction to your breakup with Jen? I don't want to enable a hasty decision."

"I'm not heartbroken or anything like that," he says with frustration and a tinge of annoyance that I might consider him so weak. "But it's partly because of Jen, yes."

"How so?"

"Do I need to tell you? I just want you to twist my lauvan or whatever you do."

I cross my arms.

"If you want my help, you'll have to be more forthcoming. I'm not irrevocably messing with your head on a whim. It's my way or the highway, I'm afraid."

Cecil sighs explosively.

"Fine. Yes, Jen is the reason I want to forget. But it's not because I'm sad we're not together. It's because every life I live, I am tangled up in this ridiculous love triangle between her, me, and Alejandro. I hate it. Most of the time I'm the other man. Who wants that? I want to break free of the cycle." He mashes his fist in his palm and paces the sidewalk. "I want to be my own man, make my own decisions, but when I remember everything, it stains my view on relationships. I want a clean slate. I want to go back to the person I was before I met Jen. I was happy. I had my life ahead of me. The world was full of potential, and any girl I met might be the one. Now, all I know is Jen and her past selves, and any other relationship I consider is tainted by that knowledge."

Cecil breathes heavily and turns away. I let the silence mellow.

"I also don't want to know about magic and elementals," Cecil blurts out. "I was happier in ignorance. There isn't much I can do about it anyway, so I might as well not know."

"You're always an asset," I say quietly. "But I understand if it's too much. You aren't the first person to react in that way, and you won't be the last." I take a deep breath. "I'm content with your reasons, and I will willingly change your memory, if that's what you wish. But not today. Sleep on it for a few days. Come back to me then, and if you haven't changed your mind, I will do it."

Cecil tightens his lips.

"Not today?"

"Not today."

He exhales.

"Okay. I'll be back."

Cecil turns and walks down the sidewalk. I watch him go, pondering the intricate connections the group of us have managed to weave during our centuries together.

When I go inside, Alejandro is still deep in the notebook, and Chloe continues to play her violin in Liam's room.

"I'm off," I announce. "Good luck with Liam. If you see any change in him, let me know."

Alejandro looks at our unresponsive friend, who is still sitting where I placed him.

"How much do I need to take care of him?" he asks, doubt coloring his voice. I consider Liam.

"He seems to do what you tell him to do. He's not totally catatonic, just lacking ambition to do his own thing. Perhaps remind him to eat or go to sleep. And good luck with the teenager. Blame Liam's condition on medication. Call me if you need backup."

"Will do," he says. "Don't forget to look at the spirit library tomorrow for answers. We need that protection if we're chasing after Xenia."

Minnie texts me at five o'clock to say she'll be having dinner with her recovering friend, so I'm contemplating the contents of our fridge when the apartment buzzer rings.

"Merry," Wayne's disembodied voice crackles from the wall unit when I press the intercom button. "Can I come up? Kat Lee has some more questions, and I thought it would be better if we answered together."

Officer Kat Lee is a friend of Wayne's, but she was also persistent in the investigation of my appearances at disasters a few weeks ago, until she came for answers and I demonstrated my abilities.

It was too much for her, and I haven't heard a peep since that day. It looks like she's had some time to think it over.

I buzz them in and pull the fridge open again. By the time Wayne knocks and enters, I have cold bottles of beer waiting on the coffee table. Officer Lee will probably need one.

Wayne walks into the living room closely followed by Officer Lee. She looks strange with her straight black hair loose and in jeans and a leather jacket instead of her usual uniform. The outfit certainly flatters her more. Her back is poker straight and her alert eyes flit about, showing her training. She's scouting for dangers even though it's a normal apartment and I am standing calmly in the center with my hands empty.

"Thanks for having us, Merry," Wayne says. He gestures to the couch then slumps onto it. After a moment's hesitation, Lee joins him but perches on the edge. I grab a bottle and relax into an armchair.

"Please." I wave at the beer. "Help yourself."

Wayne grabs a bottle with a sigh, but Lee doesn't acknowledge my invitation.

"I need to know more," she blurts out. "The autopsies on most of those bodies showed nothing. As far as the coroner is concerned, there is no cause of death. But there were ten of them like that. How could they all have died of unknown causes at once?" She narrows her eyes at me. "They didn't die on their own. Who should I be bringing to justice? I can't let this slide."

I take a swig of beer then swirl the contents of the bottle while I look into Lee's steely gaze. She's clearly not the kind of woman who enjoys a good mystery. She wants to find a culprit she can handcuff and place behind bars to clean up this mess in her mind. Unfortunately, my life isn't as tidy as that.

"Well?" she says. "What do you know? Should I take you in for questioning again?"

"That worked well last time, didn't it?" I say. When her eyes narrow into slits, I shrug and wiggle my fingers. "Powers, remember?"

She flinches then straightens her shoulders as if embarrassed by her reaction. Wayne interjects.

"Merry isn't the bad guy here. We know who is." He looks at me in exasperation. "Stop antagonizing Kat."

My lips twitch.

"But it's so much fun. Fine. How much do you really want to know, Officer Lee?"

"Everything," she says with thinned lips. "And Kat will do. I'm not on the clock, and I doubt that I can take any of this to work."

"That's the truth. All right, the culprit is a woman named Xenia. She is an elemental spirit who has possessed the body of March Feynman, and she has abilities like mine, although

67

greatly enhanced. She, along with her elemental followers—also possessing human bodies—came from their parallel realm into our physical world. When I and my friends tried to stop them, they retaliated with a heated battle at the bottom of Cathbar Street. We were able to defeat most of Xenia's followers, although Xenia escaped. For those possessed bodies that were not already dead, we removed the elemental and released the humans back to their lives." I look at Wayne. "Did I miss anything?"

Wayne shakes his head, a smile playing on his mouth. Kat stares at me with uncomprehending eyes.

"Spirits?" she says faintly. "Parallel realm? Possession?"

"Yes, yes, and yes," I say cheerfully. "You have it."

Kat passes a shaking hand over her eyes.

"So,' she says quietly. "What you're saying is, you murdered those people on Cathbar, you and your friends."

"Let's keep the blame squarely on me, shall we? There is no need to involve my friends. Also, you used the word 'murder,' but is it truly accurate? Would you say a soldier murdered the enemy in a war?"

"This is Vancouver," she snaps, her fire returned. "There is no war."

"Tell that to the victims," I say, my own passion emerging. I lean forward in my seat. "Gary Watson died to protect the people of this city from the threat of Xenia. Firefighters caught in the crossfire were swept away to drown in the tsunami. The only reason Vancouver isn't shaking with unmitigated natural disasters right now is from our efforts. If you want to label them as murders, fine. But I regret nothing."

I breathe heavily and stare at Kat. She searches my eyes, and I don't know what she sees there. Gary's memory deserves better than to be swept under the rug as an unfortunate accident to those who know the truth. I wish I could have announced

68

his sacrifice from the rooftops, but at least Kat should be aware.

Kat finally looks away and through the window into the dark night.

"I can't bring you in," she says quietly. "Not with a story like that, and not without evidence. I'd be laughed out of the department." She rubs her forehead. "This Xenia is still on the loose. What do you know of her whereabouts, her plans?"

I lean back in my chair and take a sip of beer. Wayne and I exchange expressive glances at Kat's acceptance of our crazy world. I doubt she fully understands or believes, not yet, but she's focusing on the relevant information which I appreciate.

"Unfortunately, too much. Have you seen the construction on Point Grey Road?" At Kat's nod, I continue. "That's the site of Xenia's new temple. She's styling herself as a reborn Aztec goddess and is recruiting followers. Given her elemental ability to brainwash anyone who comes too close, I'd classify it more as a cult than a religion. One of our friends has already succumbed, and I can't do anything to snap him out of it."

Kat sits up straight, and her eyes flash.

"A cult? Have you seen any evidence of mistreatment?"

"Xenia forces her followers to build her temple. Conditions don't look particularly safe, and her followers are abandoning their jobs and lives. She threatened bodily harm should they not obey."

"Okay, great." Kat gives a satisfied smile. "Cults I can handle. Let me talk to my captain. I'm sure we can get a team over there to investigate and shut them down."

"No," I say quickly. Wayne looks as horrified as I feel. "Don't do that. If your people get too close, Xenia can brainwash them, too. They'll be under her control. Do you understand? She can make them do anything, anything at all."

Kat's face twists in frustration.

69

"I can't just do nothing," she bursts out. "What am I supposed to do?"

I heave a sigh.

"I'm working on a solution. There isn't a lot you can do. I can protect myself against the compulsion, so let me handle it. The best thing you can do right now is give me free rein. I'll use my contacts in the other realm to fix this."

Kat squeezes her fists in her lap.

"Other realm," she mutters. "This is absurd. I don't like it, but okay. But if you fail, I'm coming after you. Got it?"

My mouth twitches in a wry smile.

"I would expect nothing less."

CHAPTER IX

Dreaming

I thrust my sword at the nearest soldier and pull his errant strands at the same time. He falls to the ground with a wheeze of pain.

"Come on, Merlin!" Beorn shouts. He stands in the doorway of the great hall of Ælla, the ruler of the Anglian kingdom of Deira. We are both men-at-arms for Ælla, and we're losing terribly to the men of neighboring Bernicia. Their king decided to invade, and there was little time to muster an army. The men of the household were the only protection Ælla and his family had. Now that the rest are captured, there is little Beorn and I can do.

"On my way," I call out and race after Beorn. We flee through back passageways into the kitchens and burst out near the stables. Its thatched roof is burning, and the panicked neighing of horses is a pitiable sound.

We run a few short steps to the stable doors, but a shout alerts others to our presence. I yank open the door and we dart inside.

Smoke is thick, and horses kick the walls of their stables with urgent thumps. I open the latch of the nearest stall, and the horse gallops out as soon as it realizes the door is open.

Eight horses escape in this way. I cough on the dense smoke, and my lungs feel as though they are drying out and cracking.

"Time to go," Beorn says hoarsely, and he reaches into the farthest stall to grab the bridle of the panicking horse. There is no way we will get on the backs of these horses, not in their current state. It's time to pull out my tricks.

The mare that Beorn attempts to control rolls her eyes at me and neighs when I look in. There is no time for finesse. I snatch a few of her twitching strands and pour calming thoughts into them. Within a moment, she quiets. Even when a piece of burning thatch drops onto the floor next to her, she merely looks at us with calm eyes and huffs.

"Get on," I yell at Beorn. He stares at me with wide eyes but does as he is told. I race to the final stall where a large brown gelding pounds the door with his hooves. After I calm him, he's ready to ride, and I follow Beorn out the door.

Spears whistle past us, but I throw up a hasty barrier of air that slows them enough so that they graze our fur-lined cloaks instead of pierce them. We thunder past, unharmed.

When we reach the relative safety of the woods, far out of sight of the burning household, Beorn stops and wheels his horse around.

"What was that?" he demands. "You used magic to calm the horses, I'm sure of it. What are you?"

I sigh. I don't want to have this conversation again. I have only lived for a century and a half, but already this feeling is too familiar. I hoped that I could travel with Beorn for longer than this, but if he is already accusing me of witchcraft, our paths will have to diverge.

Unless—I look at him in consideration. We have fought side-by-side under Ælla for many months, and a friendly camaraderie exists between us, enough so that a few strands of lauvan connect us. I grip the strands and pour my intention into them while I twist them between my fingers.

"Come down from your horse, Beorn," I say calmly. "I can make this right."

A look of unconcern passes over Beorn's face, and he slides off the mare and stands placidly by her side. I climb off my own mount and approach Beorn. I have wanted to try altering memories, and now is the perfect opportunity. With a few

72

twists, the last minutes can be erased. He will never know that he saw me perform magic, and we can carry on as before.

I deftly knot lauvan at his forehead. It doesn't take long before I am satisfied with my work. I step back and peer at him.

"Beorn. What do you remember?"

Beorn opens his mouth, but only nonsense words tumble out. He looks confused and tries again, but the same thing occurs.

Something went wrong. What did I do? I raise my hands and fiddle with his strands, desperate to fix the damage.

"Merlin?" Beorn says. "What happened? I thought we were accompanying Lady Nothgyth to the river today. Why are we in the forest?"

That is a memory from months ago. Have I erased that much? I start to sweat. This was a mistake. I took away months of Beorn's life, and I don't know how to get them back. How can improve my skills at memory manipulation when the stakes are so high? I never wanted to hurt Beorn. How can I avoid ruining my friend's life?

CHAPTER X

The next morning, I wander into the kitchen with an unsettled feeling after my dream. Minnie chops potatoes on a wooden cutting board.

"Good morning. Grab the casserole dish, will you?" she says when she sees me. "I thought I'd get a head start on dinner tonight."

"You know I don't have a casserole dish. My frying pan will have to do. It can go in the oven."

"You forget," Minnie says with a cheeky smile. "I brought my cookware with me. It's in the oven drawer."

I open the drawer with interest and find it packed with cooking implements.

"How do you even find things?" I grumble as I push pots aside in my quest. "Modern people make cooking too complicated. Do you mean this one?"

I hold up a white ceramic dish. Minnie glances at it and nods.

"That's the one. Works a charm. You'll see."

I shove the rest of the pots back into the drawer with difficulty and push it closed with my foot. I place the dish on the counter before Minnie with a flourish.

"I'll believe it when I eat it."

Minnie throws a potato at me.

"Peel this, chef Lytton. Make yourself useful."

I ignore the peeler that lies on the counter and grab my trusty paring knife. Minnie might like a thousand contraptions, but I prefer simplicity. Besides, I am adept with this little knife. To prove a point, I peel one long, spiral length from the potato and drape it across the counter. Minnie chuckles and takes the potato I hand her.

"Yes, you're a marvel. I know."

She places the potato on the cutting board and raises her knife to chop it. Her fingers are far too close to the intended cutting spot, and they are splayed out instead of curled inward for safety. I wrap my hand around her wrist to stop the motion of the knife.

"Are you trying to shorten your fingers? Here, let me."

I try to pry the knife away, but her fingers clench tightly and her strands stiffen.

"I can cut a potato," she says shortly. "I've been doing it for years and still have all my digits."

"It only takes once. Here, I can finish for you."

I reach for the knife again, but she steps back. Her strands are now straight and point at me in defense. I look at her face in question, and her eyes are narrowed in anger.

"You're smothering me," she says with barely contained fury. "Stop hovering. I'm a competent, fully functioning adult. Treat me like one, not like your little woman."

She slams the knife on the counter and strides out of the kitchen.

"I need space," she shouts back. "You need to give me some."

I stand frozen for a long moment. It isn't until the front door thuds shut that my paralysis wears off, then I wander to the dining room and sink into a chair.

Although there may be a kernel of truth to her accusations—perhaps I'm hovering more than is healthy—I'm sure that the old Minnie would not have blown up about it. Old Minnie was a calm, rational creature with a career in counseling and emotional management. New Minnie, the one that is emerging from her elemental side, is a different being altogether. I consoled her that we would work our way through it, that I would love her no matter who she becomes. I meant it, but what will the transition mean for our relationship? Can I learn

75

how to handle her new self before it drives an inalterable wedge between us?

My mood is black when I reach the university. My argument with Minnie swirls in my mind, and I can't let it go. Counterarguments surface, perfect zingers that are far too late to be useful.

I stomp into my first class, and the students look at me in alarm. I take a deep breath to compose myself. They are not to blame for Minnie's behavior, although I'd like to lay the fault elsewhere. I keep my lid on for the entirety of the morning. It's a strain.

My meeting with the Dean looms, tucked between my last morning class and the lunch hour. I stride into the department office, my dark mood still lingering. The admin glances at me with a pleased air.

"The Dean will be with you in a minute."

The admin loves to make me wait. I can see it in his strands. I itch to tweak them and make him squirm, but I resist with great difficulty. Only Minnie's indignant face stops me. Without her, am I only a petty thug? I feel lost when she is not at my side.

"The Dean will see you now," the admin says. I breeze past him to the open office door. The Dean looks up and nods at me.

"Merry, good to see you. Thanks for coming. Please, take a seat."

"What's this about?" I have no patience today for beating around the bush. I want her to tell me whatever she has planned so I can get out of here. Perhaps a dip in the lauvan network

76

will settle my nerves.

The Dean raises her eyebrows, perhaps surprised at my bluntness and lack of fawning. I expect most other sessional instructors tiptoe around the head of the department. I have been around too long to be awed by anyone.

"Right to business. That works for me. Merry, I've had complaints from students, which I have to follow up on."

"Complaints?" I'm genuinely flummoxed. "About what?"

"Certainly not about your teaching," she says warmly. "That remains stellar, as always. The problem is, your attendance is spotty. There have been multiple unexplained absences, students turning up to an empty classroom with no notice, marks handed in late, even some confidential complaints by staff."

The staff complaint was from the admin, I'm certain of it.

"I—"

The Dean puts up her hand.

"I'm sure you have wonderful, well-planned excuses. I don't want to hear them. If you had good reason for missing classes, you should have alerted the department ahead of time. If you are having personal difficulties, you have access to support channels and need only ask to receive help. I've let it slide this far only because your classes are so highly rated that they're a draw to the English department." She sighs. "But they are only good classes if the instructor shows up to give the lectures. Consider today your warning. Until further notice, you are under probation. A staff member will attend all your classes to ensure you are there as an active participant. If you miss a class without sufficient warning, your contract will be terminated." She leans forward, her eyes earnest. "Please don't make me fire you, Merry. You're an asset to this faculty. But I need reliable employees."

The word "probation" rings in my ears. If she only knew that half of my absences were because of Xenia and her murderous intentions, her reaction might be very different. Of course, I can't use Xenia in my defense. I can only fume silently on my side of the wide desk.

"If that's all," I say and stand. "I have a class to prepare."

She sighs again and nods slowly.

"That's all."

I stride out with stiff steps. The admin glances swiftly at me, but I don't give him any fodder in my expression to gauge the outcome of the meeting. Inside, I'm fuming. Who does the dean think she is, handing out ultimatums?

I could give up teaching. It has held less interest for me lately. Perhaps this is the universe giving me a sign. If only I believed in signs.

Only the thought of Minnie's reaction to my quitting prevents me from turning around and giving the dean my notice. Minnie is already disappointed in my lack of purpose. I need to keep this job to show her that I am fine, that I have ambition and drive, that I'm not lost. Because I'm not. I'm fine. Keeping this job will prove that to her.

I need to vent to someone, so I angle my heavy footsteps to Wayne's office. The door is open, and I knock perfunctorily before striding in. Wayne looks up from his position at his desk.

"Merry." He rolls back and puts his hands behind his head then peers at me with a frown. "You look like a thundercloud. What's up?"

"I'm on probation," I snarl. "The dean gave me an ultimatum, said if I don't start turning up to classes, I'm out."

Wayne's face creases with sympathy.

"Ouch. Probation is a harsh sentence."

"Yes, someone will be attending all my classes, reporting to Big Brother. Big Sister, in this case." I run my hand through my hair. "I hate being micromanaged."

Wayne places his hand on the desk and drums his fingers.

"She has a point," he says eventually. "Attending classes isn't your strong suit these days, and turning up is a big part of this gig."

"Yes, yes," I say with impatience. "I've already heard it from the dean. Turn up or get out. I'll tell that to the people Xenia planned to murder for skin suits. I'm sure they'll find comfort in it."

Wayne winces.

"True enough. Hey, tell me more about Xenia's worship meeting. Alejandro told me about Liam's condition." Wayne shakes his head. "I don't know, we're in deep waters again. You really can't undo it?"

"Both Minnie and I tried multiple times. I don't know what Xenia did, but it's unbreakable."

"What was the meeting like?"

I think back to the oceanside construction site, Xenia's costume, the blank looks of dozens of new followers.

"She has a system, for certain. As long as she can attract enough new people each meeting, she can turn each one into a follower. Skeptics or believers, it makes no difference. They all get brainwashed the same. And it's airtight, as Liam's strands show."

Wayne shakes his head again and turns to his computer.

"I want to see this for myself. If we know what she's up to, we can avoid the brainwashing portion."

"Alejandro is looking for a method of protection. But, yes, if I am with you, I can watch for the mind control. It's easy to spot, now I know what I'm looking for."

"What did she call her goddess?" Wayne says absently.

"Coatlicue."

Wayne types and clicks until he finds a rudimentary website.

79

Xenia's picture is on the top with a list of dates below.

"The next meeting is today," Wayne says. "Half an hour from now, in fact. Do you have classes?"

"Not for the rest of the day. Let's go."

The construction site is a hive of activity today. Workers swarm like bees over the earthworks, and two yellow excavators dig ceaselessly in one half of the site. In the other half, a cement foundation rises from the action of a concrete boom pump. Whatever project Xenia has in mind, it is being built swiftly.

"Are all these people her followers?" Wayne asks in awe. "The workers, I mean?"

"I expect so. She might be paying them, but they are working faster than construction workers usually do."

"That's a sweeping judgement, Merry," Wayne says reprovingly. I shake my head and point.

"You don't rush in construction. Trust me, I've done enough of it. It's not safe otherwise. Accidents happen with speed." I point at a man without a hard hat who hauls on a strap. He's precariously balanced on the foundation's edge, with the boom of the concrete pump wavering overhead. "That shouldn't be happening."

Wayne rubs his bald head in agitation.

"We should go warn him."

"They wouldn't stop and listen if we tried. Trust me, you haven't seen Liam yet. The amount of control Xenia has is unreal. The only way we're stopping her followers is by cutting the head off the snake herself. Come on, let's see what the daughter of Coatlicue has to say today."

Before we reach the main path to the flat section where Xenia held her last meeting, I pull Wayne behind a portable toilet. He wrinkles his nose.

"What are you doing?"

"Making you unrecognizable." I grab his rust-colored strands and twist them swiftly. "I don't want Xenia to see us. She knows us all by sight after the battle a few weeks ago. If she sees us, she'll target us for certain."

A few seconds later, Wayne emerges from behind the toilet sporting a full head of brown hair, a larger nose, and a baggy hooded coat. I follow and toss long black hair out of my face.

"You're quite a looker," Wayne teases. "Thought you'd try out the other sex for a bit?"

"It pays to practice." I sway my hips as I walk beside him. "The nuances of acting like a woman are not easy to master. I like to remain versatile. Besides, it's amusing to switch it up."

"I bet it is." Wayne chuckles. When he spots the meeting point, his smile fades.

More than a hundred people are crammed into the small, graveled clearing before a wooden dais. More than half of the people bear the mark of Xenia's brainwashing, but the rest do not. If Xenia carries out the same trick as last time, her numbers will swell hugely.

"And she has her construction workers too," Wayne says under his breath. "Are all these people going to drink the Kool-Aid?"

"Half already have."

"But the others haven't. How can we stop this today?" Wayne looks around for a distraction. "Too bad this is outdoors, otherwise we could pull a fire alarm or something."

"Head of the snake," I remind Wayne. "We can't give up our identities. If we take down Xenia, all these people will have no one to pull their strings and will presumably revert to their

81

former selves. But we need to remain undetected until we figure this out."

Wayne grumbles but eventually nods. When the followers hush the people around them, I look forward.

Xenia climbs the dais. Whereas before her robe was simple and in colors of brown and green, it now more closely echoes ceremonial garb of the Aztecs, or what a layperson might imagine their ceremonial attire to look like. Her calf-length purple skirt is encrusted with shells and precious nuggets of turquoise and gold. The teal, tunic-like blouse is similarly adorned, embroidered with fanciful patterns along the edge that, while perhaps not historically accurate, nevertheless impress with their detail. The outfit is topped with an elaborate headdress of peacock feathers and a rim of turquoise beads, far removed from the crown of branches she wore last time. She is embracing her role as daughter of a deity.

The work site quiets as even the people operating the excavators turn off their machines. All the workers, although they stay where they are, turn to face the dais. Xenia raises her hands.

"My people," she says in a ringing tone. "Beloved of Coatlicue, people of the earth. You are chosen to carry out her great work, and she cherishes you. Bow down before Xenia, daughter of Coatlicue, and let your eyes be opened to miracles!"

There is muttering of consternation of those in the crowd whose temple strands are not yet knotted, but Xenia's followers put hands on the others' arms and mutter reassurances.

Xenia turns and points her finger at a lump of bedrock that the excavator had been ineffectually scraping before. The pointing hand is a distraction, for the fingers of her other hand twist and pull earth lauvan while she points dramatically.

82

A deep, moaning crack of splitting rock thunders through my chest. The crowd gasps. A crevasse yawns in the bedrock, then chips fly off it. Swiftly, the rock crumbles until only a pile of rubble remains.

When the rumbling dies away, there is a pause of silence, then Xenia's followers yell and stomp their feet. The uninitiated stare at the pile in shock. Xenia turns to the crowd and raises her hands again with a calm smile. Her fingers work.

"My people," she shouts. "The power of the earth is mine, and you are my chosen ones!"

The crowd shouts and stamps louder as the effect of Xenia's lauvan manipulation spreads outward from her like a wave. I take Wayne's arm in a pincer grip and yank him backward. He stumbles along behind me until we are free of the crowd and are walking swiftly up the path. I chance a look back, but Xenia's attention is engaged with her task and she doesn't glance our way.

"What—" Wayne pants. "The hell was that?"

"Xenia in action." My face is set in grim lines. "Just like that, she has another fifty followers, replicas of Liam."

"We need to stop her," Wayne says. "Drop me off at the spirit library on the way. Anna's there right now. We need answers, and that's the only place we know where to look."

83

CHAPTER XI

Alejandro texts me before we leave the construction site, so I drop Wayne off at the apartment that I rented to stash the spirit library.

"I'll come back later," I tell Wayne. "As soon as I try untangling Liam again. Alejandro thinks he found a solution."

"I'll call you if I find anything," Wayne says. "There's a lot there, though. How many IKEA shelves did you order to house all the books?"

"Enough to warrant a delivery truck."

Wayne chuckles then sobers.

"Does everyone know to avoid the temple site? Have we warned everyone? I don't want us to have another Liam on our hands."

"I think everyone knows." I run my hands through my hair. "No, I never told Todd."

"Your half-elemental buddy?" Wayne frowns. "Would he even be in danger?"

"I don't know if Minnie and I are immune to Xenia's lauvan manipulation, or whether we were simply far enough away. He should still know what's going on."

Once Wayne leaves the van, I text Todd with a warning to stay away from Xenia and her temple. Within seconds, he replies.

Thanks for the warning.

The last time we talked, Todd made it clear that he doesn't want to continue our acquaintance, and it looks like he hasn't changed his mind. I'm satisfied that I fulfilled my obligation. Keeping away from Xenia is up to him.

Next, I look up Vancouver's permit office. We need to slow Xenia's plans in whatever way we can, and she might not be expecting red tape. After being passed from person to person, I eventually speak to someone knowledgeable.

"We approved that project," he says blandly. "Inspectors will visit when plumbing and electricity are installed, as per specifications in building code."

"Plumbing—are you kidding me? Have you seen the monstrosity that's being built? The foundation alone is the size of four houses." The man is too blasé about this project, and an unpleasant notion steals across my mind. I ask a different question. "What do you think of Xenia?"

"Xenia, daughter of Coatlicue, performer of miracles. She is worthy to be worshiped."

It's the same answer that Liam gave, word for word. I hang up and stare at my phone with a sinking heart. Xenia has ensnared officials in the city already. How far will this madness go?

It isn't a long drive to Alejandro's, but my mind races the whole way there. The worshipful gaze of Xenia's followers bothers me, and Xenia's smug smile tells me she's getting exactly what she wants. In my experience, what Xenia wants is never beneficial to anyone but herself.

Alejandro answers quickly when I knock on the door.

"Good, you're here." He jerks his head to the couch, where Liam watches television with the sound down.

"No change?" I say quietly. Chloe is seated at the round table doing schoolwork. I relax when I see ear buds poking through her hair.

"Nothing," Alejandro says. "But I was reading grandfather's notebook, and there was a spell to protect against compulsion by the gods. It's worth a try. I did it, but nothing happened. Maybe if you untangle lauvan at the same time, it might do something."

Chloe looks up when she sees me out of the corner of her

eye.

"Hi, Merry," she says. "You're back."

"Just saying hello. Keeping up with your schoolwork?"

She rolls her eyes.

"I have to read To Kill a Mockingbird. So boring. My teacher is a total bear, though, so I have to finish it by next week."

"Ah, yes. Those English teachers who make you keep up with the readings." I maintain a straight face, but Alejandro snorts. "Terrible people."

"Totally." Chloe nods vigorously. "You get it."

"Don't let me be the cause of your digressions," I say. "Carry on with Harper Lee."

Chloe shrugs and turns her head to glance at Liam, who is behind her on the couch.

"Is he really on medication?" she asks. "Mum was on morphine when she had surgery last year, and she didn't act like that. It's like there's something wrong with him." She glances at me with a calculated gleam in her eyes. "Is he high? It doesn't smell like pot. Or is it edibles? Can I have some?"

I roll my own eyes.

"Get back to Lee," I say.

She huffs and pops her earbuds back in.

Alejandro waves me over to Liam. I stand with my back to Chloe so that my body shields him from her view. Alejandro holds up the photocopied pages of Braulio's notebook.

"Here," he whispers. "This spell."

I read it carefully. It's a short incantation in Ancient Greek. I recite it and watch Liam's temple closely.

The strands twitch, but I don't know whether that's due to the spell or random lauvan movements.

"Something happened," I say quietly. "I'll try again and untangle at the same time."

My fingers deftly grasp the loosest strands of the knot. Under my breath, I recite the incantation again and again. The strands twitch then writhe. I wiggle the strands in my grasp with careful force.

They don't budge. Alejandro must see my frustrated face, for his shoulders slump.

"Let me try again," I say through gritted teeth.

I repeat my actions and words for five minutes until I fling my hands out and run my fingers through my hair.

"It was worth a try," Alejandro says consolingly, although his strands droop in disappointment.

"It was. Back to the drawing board, I guess. I'll go help Wayne and Anna at the spirit library now."

"Umm." Alejandro glances at Chloe and back to me. "Do you think it's okay to leave Chloe with Liam? I have a date, and Liam's not exactly a great babysitter right now."

I appraise Chloe's bent head.

"She's fourteen, isn't she? I was on my own at her age." I sigh. "But these are different times. I'm sure she'll be fine, but I can stay with her for a while if it would make you feel better, or until she kicks me out."

Alejandro grins.

"Just keep her company for a bit. If she wanders off, I'll feel responsible."

"Who's the woman today?" I'm curious about Alejandro's string of dates. He has jumped into the dating pool with both feet and is now swimming laps. It doesn't surprise me. He fully embraces whatever he does.

"Her name is Lucy. She's a friend of a coworker. Besides her being my age, I don't know anything else about her." Alejandro shrugs. "We'll see. It's kind of fun, the surprise of it. I never know who I'll meet. I like getting to know new people."

I pat him on the shoulder and push him toward the front door.

"I know you do. Go on, knock her socks off."

Alejandro laughs.

"I'll be content to not bore her. I doubt anyone's socks are coming off."

"Don't rule out possibilities."

Alejandro shoves his feet into shoes, gives me a wave, and heads out the door. I pull out my phone to let Minnie know where I am. I'm careful to word it so that I don't ask her how she is doing, although I ache to know. I hate being apart from her.

I last for five minutes watching Liam's television program—some reality show about racing around the world—before I leap up from the couch and pace to the round table. I drop into a seat near Chloe. She glances at me with suspicion, dips the spine of her book to the table, and pulls out an earbud with practiced attitude.

"What?" she says.

"Alejandro asked me to stay with you if you wanted me to. But I'm bored."

"I have schoolwork to do." She waves listlessly at the book.

"It's about young Scout Finch and her lawyer father Atticus who live in a Southern US town during the Great Depression. Atticus tries and fails to defend a black laborer from a false charge of rape. The main themes are race, justice and judgment, morality and ethics, and compassion. Memorize the quote at the end of chapter three about walking around in someone else's skin, stick it in your essay, and you're golden."

Chloe blinks at me, then she slams the book closed.

"I could have used you around earlier," she says. "That was too easy."

"It's still a good book. You'll probably get more out of it in

88

a couple of years. Try reading it then."

"How do you know so much?" Chloe narrows her eyes in suspicion. I try not to smile.

"I've read it before. And I teach literature at the university."

"And you convinced me not to read it?" Her eyebrows rise.

"I told you, I'm bored."

Chloe shakes her head incredulously, then her eyes flick to the back of Liam's head.

"He's been like that the whole time," she says. Her fingers play with the cover of her book. "So weird and boring. I hope he's off his meds soon. I don't know why he didn't tell Mum about it." She sighs in the way only a disgruntled teenager can. "It's going to be such a long week. I remember Uncle Liam being way cooler than this. I thought Vancouver would be fun."

"I'm hopeful that he'll make a full recovery shortly." Hope springs eternal in the human heart, even though nothing I have tried has worked yet. "Give it a day or so, and the two of you will be sightseeing and frolicking in the rainstorms again."

Chloe snorts.

"You seem like a cool guy, then you say things like frolicking. What century are you from?"

I can't keep the grin off my face this time. I lean back in my chair to get comfortable.

"I'm old, I know."

"Hey." Chloe leans forward, and her carefully curated nonchalance slides off. "You said you could give me a violin lesson. I'm having trouble with one of my exam pieces."

I stand.

"Looks like I have something to keep me occupied after all. Where's your instrument?"

Chloe rushes to Liam's bedroom and returns with her violin. It's a standard student instrument on the higher quality end.

Chloe sets her music stand beside the round table and brings the violin to her shoulder in a familiar fashion.

"Okay, the part I'm having trouble with is in the middle. You'll hear it, it's terrible."

She draws her bow across the strings and plays. It's a waltz by Franz Liszt, whom I saw in concert once in Germany, although he performed the piano, not the violin. Chloe is very competent and has hints of passion to her playing. She is clearly enthusiastic about her music.

The music stutters at the promised spot, and she drops her bow from the strings in defeat.

"I can't get that part, no matter how slowly I go through it. What am I doing wrong?"

I hold my hands out for her instrument. She hesitates then carefully passes the violin and bow to me. I rest it at the crook of my neck. The weight of the instrument on my shoulder brings back memories of playing in Wagner's opera house. It has been many years since I have drawn horsehair across a string, but my body doesn't forget.

"Let me run through it once. It has been a while since I've played this piece."

I run my fingers up and down a scale then launch into the waltz. After the first few bars remind me of the tune, I close my eyes to better feel the piece. Music was my first profession, and it's one I have returned to again and again. Most tunes I have played still reside in my mind or are imprinted on my soul. Musical notation on the written page is a newer phenomenon, after all.

I play until the end, enjoying the feel of a violin in my hands and the rich notes that sing from it. When I finish and open my eyes, Chloe stares at me with an open mouth.

"You're really good," she breathes. "Way better than my teacher. I thought you worked at the university, not the symphony."

"I told you I'm old," I say with a straight face. "I used to play for an orchestra."

"Wow." She shakes her head in amazement. "But I still don't know how to get that one section."

"Try holding your hand at this angle." I demonstrate. "Those top notes are much easier to play like that."

"That's not what my teacher said to do," she says doubtfully.

"Yes, and you're not getting it, are you? Don't beat your head against the wall trying the same thing repeatedly if it's not working. And no one is the primary authority on anything. Learn from others then decide for yourself what to do."

Chloe nods in thought. I offer the violin back to her, and she brings it to position.

"From the top," I say. "And remember that angle."

Chloe plays. In a few spots, she adds some vibrato where she hadn't before, and I realize she's imitating my rendition. At the troublesome spot, her hand adjusts slightly. The top notes sing out, clear and strong, and her mouth twitches with pleasure. She continues to the end but when it is finished, she grins. I nod.

"You did it."

"That was great. You have no idea how long I've been playing that bar for." She rustles her music. "I have another trouble spot. Can you look at it for me?"

I open my mouth to answer, but movement from the couch distracts me. Liam leans forward, turns the television off with the remote control, then stands. Without a word to either of us, he walks to the hall closet and shrugs on his coat then slides into his shoes and opens the front door.

"Liam," I say loudly. "Where are you going?"

"Out," he says. I stride swiftly to him and grab his arm.

"I don't think you should be going out in your state," I say.

He looks calmly at my hand on his arm, then peels back the fingers with enough force to cause damage unless I remove them. When I release his arm, he walks through the doorway. The door slams shut behind him, pushed by the wind outside, and Chloe and I look at each other.

"Should he be walking around if he's high on meds?" Chloe asks.

"Probably not. But he seemed determined."

Chloe looks longingly at her instrument.

"I really wanted to keep practicing."

"You can stay here, and I'll chase Liam down." That would be best to avoid awkward questions if I must force Liam back in his brainwashed state. Is Xenia calling him? Is he under her compulsion? I wonder what Liam is capable of as a puppet of Xenia.

"I don't want to stay here by myself," she declares. "It's creepy being alone. I'll come with you. Can we continue our lesson later?"

"Of course. But perhaps you should stay. I won't be long."

"Nope." She juts her chin out. "I'm coming. You can't make me stay."

"Fine." Perhaps it is better if Chloe comes. Then I can fulfill my promise to Alejandro to keep an eye on her. If some force is needed to get Liam in line, I'm practiced at hiding my motions from spectators. I swiftly shrug on my coat. "Quickly, now. Liam is getting away."

Chloe slides on her boots and pulls a raincoat over her sweatshirt. Together, we race out the front door.

Liam is already three blocks away when we reach the sidewalk. The rain has started in earnest, and gusty wind blows water into our faces. Chloe wrinkles her nose and pulls her hood closer around her face.

"Let's run," I say. "Catch up with Liam."

My feet pound the pavement, and Chloe's footsteps follow me. Although Liam walks with a relentless gait, it doesn't take long for us to catch up. Chloe tugs on his sleeve.

"Uncle Liam?" she says in a higher voice than usual. "Where are you going? Come back to the house."

"I must contribute," he says in a flat tone. "There is so much to be done."

Chloe and I exchange a worried glance. I look at Liam's forehead as we trot at his side. The knotted strands pulse. It's as I feared. Xenia has him under her sway, and there is a compulsion on him to walk. And from the direction his steps take him, I can guess where he's going.

I pull Chloe back so we follow Liam a few paces behind.

"This isn't uncommon with some medication side effects." I'm lying through my teeth, but Chloe is young enough to not know better. "This compulsion to move. We could force him home, but it's probably best to let him walk it out. Good for him to get exercise, anyway."

Chloe stares at Liam's back then looks up at the gray sky.

"Does he really have to walk in a storm?"

"You can go back if you like. I don't mind following him to make sure he is safe. Why don't you return and work on that piece we were practicing?"

"No." Chloe shivers and tucks her hands in her pockets. "I'll come."

After fifteen minutes of walking, Chloe is irritable, and I breathe deeply to keep my patience.

"How far are we going to let him walk? I didn't bring any money for a cab home. My shirt is getting wet now, this stupid coat is terrible."

"If you want to go back, no one is stopping you." So much for my attempt at patience. I exhale. "I can give you cab money."

"No, it's fine."

"Then keep your complaints to yourself."

Chloe grumbles, but quietly enough that I can ignore her. Liam stalks ahead, his strides unending. Luckily, the construction site is only two blocks away. For better or for worse, we will find out what happens to Liam. Hopefully, I can keep him from trouble.

We round the corner and I stop in amazement. Earlier today, there was only a cement foundation at the base of the cliff. Now, hours later, walls of stone are crawling up the embankment. The footprint of the structure is easily the size of four mansions put together, and the height is growing to match.

Excavators still dig around the perimeter, although their numbers are being replaced by flatbeds carrying huge blocks of granite and towering crane trucks. In addition, hundreds of workers swarm the site, some with shovels, some with picks, and some with wheelbarrows. There is a line of workers carrying stones in their arms from a dump truck to the rising walls of the structure. Other workers slap mortar on previously laid stones and place the new arrivals on top.

Liam marches forward, picks up a cut piece of plywood from the ground, and joins a group of workers at a mound of dirt. He pushes dirt onto the plywood with his bare hands and uses the wood to transfer soil into a nearby wheelbarrow. Every worker surrounding him shares his vacant expression.

"What the hell is this?" Chloe whispers to me. She darts forward toward Liam, and I only just manage to grab the back of her raincoat.

"Stop," I hiss. "There's more going on than you know. Don't single Liam out. You might put him in danger."

At the word "danger", Chloe stops struggling. She stares at her uncle for a long moment, then she turns to me with confusion and fright in her eyes.

"Tell me what's going on," she says. "Right now."

I should have left her at the house. Chloe has no need to know about any of this, but there is no way to explain Liam's behavior unless I tell her the truth, or at least part of it. I hope Liam can forgive me for broadening his niece's worldview.

"There is a woman named Xenia who styles herself as the daughter of an Aztec goddess," I say. I will tell Chloe the bare minimum of what she needs to know and hope that it is enough. "She is not, but she does have supernatural powers."

Chloe's jaw drops, then her adolescent skepticism kicks in.

"Stop bullshitting me," she snaps. "What's really going on here?"

"Believe it or not," I say calmly. "I am explaining the truth. Xenia has put a compulsion on these people, including Liam, so that they will work for her. Liam has no choice. Alejandro and I are doing our best to break Liam free of the compulsion and stop Xenia."

Chloe's eyes are hard.

"I don't believe you."

"Fine," I say, losing patience with her, with Xenia, with the whole situation. "Liam got a new job. He's decided construction is his calling, not teaching English as a second language. It was time for him to come to work, so he left. Despite being on his meds, he still has physical capabilities, and he didn't want to miss a day of work. Is that a more palatable story?"

Chloe's eyes fill with tears, and I regret my harsh words.

"Now I don't know what to believe," she bursts out.

I open my mouth to answer, then a familiar figure walks in front of the new stonework. It's one of Xenia's minions that survived the battle a few weeks ago. His dyed blond hair atop dark skin is unmistakable. Xenia left with two air elementals in human bodies. They must be her seconds-in-command.

95

I grab Chloe's arm and turn her to walk swiftly away. She stumbles after me.

"Don't say anything," I hiss. "There's someone there who might recognize me. It will go badly for us if he does."

To her credit, Chloe swallows her angry retort until we are out of sight of the construction.

"How will we get Uncle Liam back?" she says in a small voice.

"I'm doing everything I can. Come on, I'll take you home."

We walk back to Liam's house. Chloe is shivering before we are halfway there, but she doesn't complain the entire way home.

Alejandro looks up from his reclined position on the couch. Something in our faces must alert him to the problem, for he jumps up.

"What's wrong?" he asks. Chloe sniffs and walks to Liam's bedroom then slams the door shut. Alejandro turns bewildered eyes to me.

"Liam took off," I say heavily. "Under Xenia's compulsion, he walked all the way to the construction site and started digging at the dirt with his bare hands. Chloe and I followed him. I told Chloe about how Xenia has powers of compulsion, and how she is forcing people to work for her." I know Chloe is listening, so I make certain to only say aloud what I told her. Alejandro has known me long enough to understand what I'm telling him, and I know he won't explain any more to Chloe.

"Okay." Alejandro looks worried but resolved. "I'll take care of Chloe until Liam gets back. Surely Xenia won't make them work all night, and the sun sets in an hour."

"Call me when he arrives. Otherwise, I'll go to the site again and try to get him away. I really don't think it will work, though. Xenia has her claws in him tighter than a squirrel with a nut."

It's well after the dinner hour when I get home, but the thought of Liam toiling for Xenia turns my stomach. Minnie still isn't home, although she texted me to say she would be late. The notice is more than I expect today, but it still stings that she isn't here. I don't reply, even though my fingers itch with the desire. She wants space, so I will give it to her. If being clingy is driving her away, then I must prove to her that I have given up my overprotective ways.

Instead, I put the casserole in the oven, pull Braulio's notebook off the bookshelf, and slump onto the couch. Alejandro has already combed through it, but perhaps I can see something that he has missed. I have a different vantage since I can imagine the results of lauvan manipulation better than he can.

I scan Braulio's notes with single-minded zeal. Halfway through the familiar text, a ritual jumps out at me. It could work, but it must be done when the brainwashed people are actively worshiping. I pull out my phone and visit Xenia's sparse website. The date for the next meeting of miracles is tomorrow. I must be there to try my new ritual.

Xenia is my primary purpose right now, and I must channel all my energy into defeating her. Liam's fate, toiling ceaselessly to boost Xenia's ego, weighs down my shoulders with responsibility. He, and too many others like him, rely on me to get out of this mess. If I had defeated Xenia once and for all at the elemental battle, they wouldn't be in this predicament.

The thought of purpose makes me glance at the table where the results of my personality test lie undisturbed. I still don't know what to make of them. If I defeat Xenia, and if I survive the encounter, which I hope I will, I wonder what I will do with my life. Despite the dire predicament she is forcing on my friend, Xenia is a welcome distraction to funnel my energy.

Minnie can't possibly say I am aimless now, not when I am trying to prevent Xenia performing her destructive habits.

Minnie finally opens the front door. I stay in my seat on the couch, wanting desperately to leap to my feet and sweep her into an embrace, but nervous of how she would react. Before this week, I wouldn't have hesitated.

"Hi," she says when she comes around the corner.

"Hi, yourself." I aim for casual interest. "Did you have a good day at work?"

"Yes, thanks."

She bustles around, hanging up her coat and getting a drink from the kitchen. I stay in my spot on the couch, pretending to read a book but really focusing on holding my casual position. Finally, Minnie flops on the cushion beside me.

"I popped by Inna's on the way home," she says in a normal voice. "She wants to throw a party for us next week because we got married. She's a little miffed that she wasn't a witness, I could tell." Minnie waves her hands around, indicating that she saw Inna's strands signal her emotion. "But she can't refuse an excuse to get together. She'll be recovered by next week. Do you care what day?"

"You two decide." I kiss her cheek. "I'm easy."

"I know you are," she says with a grin then yawns. "I'm beat. Almost ready for dinner?"

I'm happy that she is acting normally. It's a strain to pretend that the tension of earlier has dissipated, but for the sake of Minnie's attempt to ignore her changing personality, I'm happy to play along.

"Whenever you are."

CHAPTER XII

Dreaming

The conductor taps his baton on the podium.

"Gentlemen," he says quietly, but the acoustics are good enough that everyone in the orchestra can hear him easily. "Tonight, Richard Wagner himself will be in the audience, in this, his new opera house. I expect the very best from each one of you."

He gazes around impressively, as if we haven't heard him give a similar admonishment a dozen times before. I shift impatiently in my seat. I don't care if Wagner is watching, or napping, or fondling his mistress in the back. All I want is to lose myself in the music.

We're playing the second opera of *Der Ring des Nibelungen* tonight, and my fingers itch to draw my bow across my violin. It's an interesting instrument to play, for its range and ability to achieve soulful notes. Although the harp was my first instrument and will always hold a special place in my heart, I'm rather fond of the violin.

I had no interest in being first violin—far too much fame and responsibility—so I downplayed my skills during my audition. I am happily ensconced as second violin beside my colleague Torben, who has earned the recognition more than I have.

The conductor raises his baton for the overture, and I bring my bow to the instrument. Before I lose myself in the music, I reflect on my long history as a musician, and how my life turns in great cycles with repeating motifs. I hope that is true with other aspects of my life. I would dearly love to see Arthur again, as he promised.

My friend Leonard throws me a bottle of bourbon. I only catch it thanks to centuries of training and honed reflexes despite my inebriation. It's lucky I do, for the bottle is hard to come by in these Prohibition days, but Leonard is rich enough to have a full cellar.

"Good catch, Marty!" Leonard crows. The flapper girl hanging onto his shoulder giggles with drunken interest. The fringe on her beaded dress sways as she leans into Leonard. He grins and wraps an arm around her waist.

I uncork the bottle with a satisfying pop and take a swig. It's smooth going down—as it should be, given the price tag—and I smack my lips in appreciation. The woman next to me, Effie, takes the bottle from my hand.

"Got to love New York in the spring," she says with a drawl. When she tips the bottle back, a peacock feather in her headband tickles my neck.

I look across the large hotel suite, filled with young, fashionable people, and wonder what I'm doing here. In a good mood, nineteen-twenties Manhattan is the height of fun and frivolity. There are plenty of sociable young men wanting to live the high life, and many young ladies willing to dance and drink with them. I enjoy being the life of the party, or at minimum on the exuberant outskirts, but the smooth burn of bourbon makes me question my time here.

Everything feels so aimless. I've been wandering for so long. My previous wife died over a hundred years ago. Am I too old and jaded for love? Perhaps Celeste was my last heart-song.

I gently push Effie away from me and stand. Effie looks at me with a question in her eyes, but I don't bother answering.

100

The booze, Effie, this whole party makes me sad and disgusted. I need to get out of the city and try something new. Perhaps if I'm a better man, a better woman might take pity on me and allow me to love her.

I can only hope.

My eyes blink blearily awake. It's still dark out, but Minnie's soft breathing comforts me. My hand reaches out to touch her shoulder to remind myself that she's truly here, but I stop before I make contact.

I don't want to wake her up and appear too clingy. I appreciate—more than she can ever know—having her in my life to give it form and substance. I don't wish to jeopardize that by smothering her.

My hand itches with my desire to feel her warm skin, but I resist.

CHAPTER XIII

Xenia's miracle meeting is at noon today. If I leave class twenty minutes early, I will have time to drive to the site. My plans evaporate when I enter my first lecture room and see a staff member in the back of the class. She smiles at me and I nod stiffly back. How can I get to the meeting on time? I need to be there when Xenia's followers are actively worshiping her. Perhaps if I fly to the site, I will be quicker.

I curse my bad luck and push through my classes doggedly. My last class is reading Shakespeare's *Cymbeline*, and I choose a few students to act the parts aloud for my own amusement.

"By Jupiter, an angel!" The young man spits in his fervor. I strain to keep a calm countenance at his antics. "Or, if not, an earthly paragon! Behold divineness no elder than a boy!"

"Good masters, harm me not," a young woman intones as she stares at her book. She has decided to dampen her enthusiasm until we all fall asleep, no doubt. I tune out for a moment and restrain my foot from tapping impatiently on the floor while she speaks.

"All gold and silver rather turn to dirt!" a different student recites. "As 'tis no better reckon'd, but of those who worship dirty gods."

I glance at the clock on the wall. All this talk of worshiping and dirt is making me antsy. Xenia's meeting is starting in ten minutes, and I'm still stuck in the classroom. The staff member looks at me with patient attention. What can I say that will excuse me with cause?

"Any further questions?" I ask the class. When they shake their heads, I say, "We're doing well, according to the syllabus. Shall we forge ahead with our next work, even though you likely haven't pre-read the text, or would you prefer the chance to leave early and catch up on your readings?"

The class murmurs their agreement with the second option, and the students pack their bags. The staff member narrows her eyes, but there isn't much to complain about. She doesn't have to know that I had planned to discuss *Cymbeline* at more length.

I walk sedately out of the classroom, but as soon as I am away from prying eyes, I run for the door. In a tucked-away corner of the building outside, I yank on my strands. A breathless moment later, I'm flapping my wings skyward as a merlin falcon. It's the quickest way to reach the construction site.

It takes me only a dozen minutes to fly to the site through the ever-present rain, but I worry it is too long. Both meetings that I attended were short, only long enough for Xenia to say a few words and tweak lauvan to manipulate her followers' minds. I flap harder, determined to make it. Once again, I consider quitting my job. There are more important things to do with my time. Minnie's admonishing face swims in my mind's eye, and I discount the notion.

When the construction site appears through nearby trees, I almost droop in relief. A crowd of people is gathered on the flat spot by the dais, clearly still in a meeting. I swoop to the ground and fly behind a tree. Once transformed to my human body, I hastily pull enough strands to change my appearance to a different-faced version of myself then run for the path.

I'm too late. Vacant-eyed people trudge their way up the gravel. The meeting is done, the people are brainwashed, and no one is actively worshiping anymore. My opportunity is lost, and my fists clench in anger. If only the dean hadn't given me probation, I could have left my class early enough to catch the worship session. I can't try my new method until the next time,

103

and that leaves Liam enthralled to Xenia for another day.

I stomp back to the sidewalk, my anger at the dean transferring to myself for missing so many classes in the first place. Then I shake my head. I only missed them because of Xenia. She is the one behind my failures. She should shoulder the blame. And, when I figure out how, she will be the one to shoulder the consequences.

I turn to stare at the construction site. Even overnight, the building has risen higher. It now towers four levels and boasts an arched entryway wide enough for five people to walk through with outstretched arms. Graceful pillars soar from ground to eave to support the roof. Everything is constructed from stone, a medley of colors giving the structure a mottled look that is pleasing to the eye. Half of the structure is carved into the rocky cliffside, and the rest pushes outward from the bedrock as if it has always been there.

The surrounding ground, now that the excavators have left, is being transformed into a landscaped stone terrace. It's only partly done and covered with workers laying flagstones, but a geometric pattern in the shape of a peaked mountain is forming in the center.

It's not hard to see that Xenia is building herself a place of worship. I still don't know what she gains from this, beyond an ego boost.

"Disgusting, isn't it?" a gruff voice says beside me. I turn to look at the newcomer. The old man's eyes are clear and keen, a far cry from Liam's vacant gaze. "Ostentatious. Some people have no sense of building their houses in keeping with the neighborhood."

"It is very strange," I agree. "Have you heard what it's going to be?"

"It's a temple, believe it or not." The man huffs his disgust, and his dog whines on its leash. "Hush, Rusty. You've heard

104

about the woman calling herself a goddess, and not the pin-up type. She has money to feed her delusions, and she's building this monstrosity using the sheep who follow her." He waves at the workers. "I don't know what kind of magnetism she's giving off, but it must be strong. All the coffeeshops and offices nearby are empty because everyone started working at the construction site."

"Do they really think she's a goddess?"

The man scoffs.

"What does that even mean? With enough people worshiping, even I could be a goddess." The man laughs. "I'm glad I have a mind like a steel trap. I'd never get conned. There are a lot of suckers in the world, the type who would send their money to a so-called Nigerian prince if they got the right email. That's not me."

"I didn't realize all the offices were emptying." Xenia's reach is greater than I thought.

"City council will have to do something about it soon. This section of the city is shutting down. I don't know, the state of the world these days…"

The man wanders off, still muttering to himself. His dog leads him away with eagerness.

Xenia's influence is spreading. I'll have to come back at the next worship meeting, job or no.

I fly back to the university, depressed and unsure where to turn next. Tonight, I might go to the spirit library and join Wayne and Anna's search of the books there. Perhaps, in all the collected works of the world's religions, there is a mention of how to get rid of an elemental brainwashing. I'm not hopeful, but until I make it to a worship session of Xenia's, it's all I can do.

The afternoon is long and tedious. I read essays because I told my class, with the staff member watching, that I would hand them back tomorrow. If I don't meet my own deadline, there will be repercussions. The dean was clear about that.

I slog through them, and by end of day I have a stack of corrected papers on my desk. The completed work brings me no joy, but at least I have a job for another day which will make Minnie content.

She's at home when I arrive, and my heart beats faster at the sound of her humming in the kitchen. I enter gingerly, unsure where we stand now. When she hears me, she turns. My shoulders slump in relief at the sight of her smile.

"Merry," she says. "Come taste this. Did I put too much cheese in it?"

I sweep toward her and thread my arms around her waist. Her neck gets a kiss before I open my mouth for her spoon of broccoli soup.

"There's never such thing as too much cheese," I say after I swallow. "It's perfect."

Minnie smiles and kisses my lips.

"Good. Dinner's ready when you are."

We sit at the dining room table, and it feels like everything is back to normal. I know I need to tell Minnie about my lack of progress with Xenia, but for a few minutes we speak of wonderfully normal things. She describes her day, and I compliment her soup. She rubs my foot under the table, and I tweak one of her strands to make her grin.

Finally, I can't put it off any longer.

"Liam is still under Xenia's spell. I can't budge it. Even an incantation that Alejandro found didn't break the knot."

Minnie sighs and puts her spoon down.

"Is he eating and sleeping? Do we need to have him committed for his safety?"

"Alejandro says he takes care of himself. Doesn't do much else, but he does do that. The poor niece is stuck there with him. We had to tell her about Xenia's powers—she followed Liam to the construction site—so fair warning if you see her. On the plus side, we don't have to hide from Chloe."

"Oh, poor girl." Minnie plays with her bread. "I wonder if I should bring her to my office during the day. Do you think it would help? I could at least see her between patients."

"I think she's fine where she is. Liam might be useless right now, but he's still family. She's safe there, and Alejandro is around." I take a last bite of soup and push my bowl to the side. "I searched for a solution to the brainwashing problem in Braulio's notebook, and I might have found one."

Minnie's eyes grow bright with interest, but she allows me to continue.

"It's another incantation, but I need to do it when Xenia's followers are actively worshiping her. I missed today's session, unfortunately, but there's one tomorrow. I will make it happen." I sit up straighter. "Xenia is indirectly my problem, and I'm going to be the solution."

"And I'll be with you. We'll take her down together." Minnie smiles warmly. "I like seeing you with some passion again. You suit purposeful."

I smile back and touch her hand. It took Xenia's ego trip to give me enough purpose to suit Minnie, but I'll take it. Hearing her say that we'll work together, after the last few days of strife, warms my heart.

"I do think," she says after she squeezes my hand in return. "This is getting out of hand. Out of our hands, specifically. We should talk to the elementals. There must be a way to deal with this brainwashing. Surely, Ailu or Shannon will know something that can help."

Last time I wanted to rely on the air elemental Ailu's help, he told me that they had enough problems of their own and not to expect anything from the elemental plane. I'm not hopeful

107

that contacting Ailu will bring results, but in the interest of keeping the peace, I nod.

"It's worth a try. Let's see if Ailu is available."

I walk to the balcony and slide the door open. Cold air blasts through the gap.

"I'm getting coats," says Minnie. After I step out and start looking for air cables, she returns with my raincoat and a sweater for herself. We slip them on, and I hold out my hands. When enough air strands filter through my outstretched fingers, I grab them and send out my intention to meet Ailu.

Within a minute—a cold, wet minute—an air cable flops from the dark sky and lands in my hand with a feeling of motion and wind passing over my palms. A figure blooms from the cable, but it isn't Ailu's voice who answers.

"Merry Lytton," the voice says. It is the low roar of a hurricane, not the raspy hoarseness of Ailu's breezy tones. An overwhelming feeling passes over me. It's the jaw-dropping power of a tornado, the relentless rush of the jet stream, and a million tiny air currents shivering through the lungs of every animal on Earth. The power of this elemental is unlike any I have yet experienced. Ailu is a gentle sigh compared to this. The voice continues, "Fetch a candle and light it. We must speak with you."

Minnie squeaks then disappears through the balcony door. I find my voice.

"Who are you? Where is Ailu?"

"We need to speak with you. Ailu can wait. Elementals know their place."

"I got it," Minnie gasps behind me. She strikes a match behind cupped fingers—she must have brought matches with her when she moved in, because I don't own any—and lights a pillar candle. It flickers furiously until she drops it into a glass hurricane lantern.

108

Immediately, the flame steadies and grows until a small lauvan figure made of sparking orange strands wavers on top of the candle. I watch in fascination. I haven't seen a fire elemental since Anna's summoning in the spring, the very first time I learned that elementals existed. I hadn't thought to summon one myself from a flame.

The fire elemental brings with it the same power as the air elemental, but this time I am bombarded by sensations of furious wildfires, erupting volcanoes, and sharp lightning from every storm currently raging on Earth. It is Fire personified, just as the other elemental typifies Air.

"Merry Lytton, son of Earth," says the fire elemental in a bright voice. "And Minnie Dilleck, daughter of Water. We meet at last."

"That's not an ominous line," I mutter. Minnie prods me with a foot. I clear my throat. "Who are you? And why the urgency for you both to speak to me? What am I to you?"

"We are the fundamentals of air and fire," the air elemental says. Minnie gasps, and my mind reels in shock. My first thought recalls Xenia and the destruction a fundamental can wreak. These two, however, have not possessed any human bodies, and from all accounts wish to remain in the elemental plane. I glance at Minnie in fear. Unless...

"Are you here to possess Minnie and I?" I say bluntly. I don't want to mince around if that is their aim. Fire chuckles.

"Fear not, son of earth. You would be a terrible vessel for me. In any event, I have no desire to enter your world."

"Why are you here? I thought being in the human world upset the balance too much."

"And it does," Fire says. "But if we limit our interaction to a quick conversation from the threads of the world, the damage will be minor. It is an acceptable risk, for we must speak with you."

109

"Why?"

What could the ruling entities of another plane of existence possibly want with a lowly half-elemental living on Earth? I have never pretended to be of importance to anyone but myself and my friends.

Air answers.

"Even if we can retrieve the earth fundamental—"

"We call her Xenia," I say.

"Even if Xenia comes back to our plane, she cannot remain the earth fundamental. It is not her fault, but she was born into captivity. Her state of half-dormancy was not a choice, and it twisted and corrupted her. She has never known the delight of joining in unity with her fellow fundamentals. There is great power there, but all parties must recognize they are part of a whole. She is filled with resentment and bitterness toward us, and that taint will never allow her to embrace her role."

"What are you saying?" Minnie says in a hushed tone.

"We need a new earth fundamental," Fire says. "It is the only way. Xenia will be stripped of her position and placed into dormancy, to be cycled through the lower echelons until she can work her way up, if she desires it."

I shake my head, trying to comprehend this news.

"I didn't know that could happen," I say. "So, you can pick a new fundamental? That sounds simple."

"It is anything but," Air says. "A new fundamental can be made, but it takes time, and time is something we do not have. Xenia's antics have upset the balance of the world. Our plane has been in turmoil for some time, but now it is leaking to your side. Have you noticed the typhoons, wildfires, and raging ocean waves of late? Those are no coincidences. Without a fundamental to act as a conduit for elementals to flow through, energy spirals out of control. The world is out of balance, and we need an earth fundamental to set it right."

"So, who will it be?" I ask. "You should instate him or her pronto."

"It is you," says Fire simply. "As the son of the previous earth fundamental, you are the only favorable choice."

CHAPTER XIV

I stare at the orange strands for a long moment, then at Minnie's wide eyes. The words take a moment to sink in, then a wild laugh bursts out of me.

"You're kidding, right? Me. But—" I look at the fundamentals then at Minnie again. "I'm only a half-elemental. Xenia can wipe her feet on me, she has so much power. There's no way I'm capable of being a fundamental."

"If Xenia is defeated, her power can transfer to you, since you are the appropriate vessel for it."

"Defeating Xenia, there's the rub," I say. "Good luck with that."

"We agree," Fire says with a sigh. "Xenia is powerful, especially sequestered in your world and out of the reach of our full powers. We can only help through our elemental emissaries, otherwise we risk disrupting the balance and causing more harm than good. The water fundamental must come out of half-dormancy at the final moment to complete this task." Fire's head turns to look at Minnie, who twitches at the notice. "The balance must be maintained, and Water cannot come until Xenia's power is ready to be transferred. Minimal disruption, you see. Water is ready and waiting for the right moment. When Water is restored to full power, the three fundamentals can join forces to remove Xenia from the physical world. Speak with the river elemental. She will know more."

"We debated for many long weeks about the correct course of action," says Air. "But earth needs a fundamental to right the balance. With Water reinstated and Earth checked, the four will be in balance and the world will emerge from chaos, tempered but stable."

"This is insane," I mutter to myself. To the fundamentals, I say, "Assuming this is the only way, et cetera, do I have to give up my human body and live in the other plane? Because I tried that once, and I wasn't keen on it."

That is a mild understatement. I had a bodiless panic attack and possessed the nearest person to avoid free-floating in the lauvan as an elemental. Besides which, I would have to leave Minnie behind, and we have already established that isn't what either of us want. My hand searches for Minnie's, and she grips it tightly.

"No," says Air. "Even if you wanted to, it is not possible. Your human and elemental strands are too tightly intertwined. However, we can make it work."

"The important point," says Fire. "Is that someone of the correct lineage becomes the earth fundamental. And that they are willing to become part of a greater whole, not strive for their own goals. Currently, you are the only one who can do this in time to halt the spreading chaos."

"I've never been much of a team player," I say to stall. My mind is spinning twice as fast as usual, but it's getting less accomplished. What does this mean for me? Is this truly what I need to do to stop Xenia? Can I stay in my own body with Minnie and perform my fundamental role at the same time?

"As long as you are willing to try," says Air. "Xenia is not."

"Once the water fundamental is restored," Fire says. "And Xenia weakened, the three of us can remove her from the physical world. Then, you may ascend into your power."

"But before that day, you must train." Air adds. "There are initiations and stretches you must endure before your body and threads will be ready to receive the power. We will send trusted earth elementals to prepare you. The role is less of a conscious command and more of an innate one, but you must be ready. Have your answer for when they arrive. It is your choice to

113

become a fundamental. The role will give you power beyond your imagination, but if you do not become the fundamental, the world will crumble into ruin."

The two lauvan forms sink into their elements. I let go of the air cable and rub my face. Minnie pinches the candle to extinguish it.

"My choice," I mutter. "Sure. Choose wrongly and the world crumbles."

"What are you thinking about all this?" Minnie asks quietly. I glance at her pale face, but her expression only shows concern.

"I don't know." I rub both hands through my hair. "It's insane. Completely insane." I step back and lean against the outer wall of our apartment. The cold of the cement seeps through my raincoat. "But it could make sense. If I am the son of the fundamental, and the others can prepare me enough to take on the power, then we can finally defeat Xenia. She's getting too strong. I have the feeling that Vancouver is her guinea pig. Today, the city, tomorrow, the world."

"And don't forget the natural disasters that are getting worse," Minnie murmurs. I nod my agreement.

"If I can take on this role and stabilize the world while getting rid of Xenia, I don't see how I can pass it up." I exhale sharply. "And it doesn't have to be forever. If I hate it, the fundamentals said they can prepare another elemental to take over."

"There's your backup plan." The side of Minnie's mouth twitches once. I shrug.

"It never hurts to have one handy."

We stare into the rainy, windswept night. I cross my arms over my chest to ward off the cold and my heavy thoughts.

My gut reaction to the fundamentals' announcement was one of liberty, strange as it sounds.

114

Despite my outward reservations, the notion of becoming the earth fundamental feels right, especially if I can stay in my human form with Minnie at my side. I yearn for new horizons—novelty is always welcome to relieve the monotony of my overlong existence—and the elemental plane has called to me ever since I first beheld the fire elementals at Wallerton's volcano. This is a way to learn more about my heritage, my abilities, and my father's people without the panic-laden experience of being without a body.

Another enticement takes root in my chest. The thought that I might become a part of something greater than myself holds some novelty, too. For centuries, I looked out for number one because that was all I had. Now, I have a chance to contribute to the balance of the world by working with other fundamentals to maintain order. The notion of having a powerful reason to continue my days is mesmerizing.

"If I say yes," I say to Minnie. "Then you don't have to worry about finding me a purpose. I'll have one thrust upon me."

Minnie finds my hand and squeezes it.

"Come inside," she says. "It's freezing out here."

Minnie pulls me to the couch, and I clutch her tightly while she rests her head on my shoulder. I'm cold to my core, but her heat slowly thaws me. She traces her finger over my chest.

"What would being the fundamental mean?" Minnie asks. "In practice."

"I have no idea." My mind ponders the possibilities. "Do I spend part of my time in the other plane? Will always I be plugged into the lauvan network, only half-paying attention to the world around me? Will I have to travel to visit tectonically active sites?"

"These are good questions to ask the earth elementals that are coming. Make sure you know what you are getting into."

I stroke her hair with gentle fingers. This decision affects her, too.

"Do you think I should do it?"

Minnie is silent for a long time. I continue to stroke her hair, not wanting to rush her thoughts. She finally sits up and lays her hand on my jaw.

"I do," she says. "I think this is what you have needed for an exceedingly long time. It will change your life in ways we can't imagine yet, but I think it will be for the better. It will be rough to start—transitions always are—but when you find your groove, you will wonder how you lived without it."

"You've been reading *Finding Your Purpose*, haven't you?" I give her a wry smile then sigh and draw her down into my arms again. She settles back on my shoulder. "I'll sleep on it and ask my questions of the elementals, but I think you're right."

"I usually am," she murmurs. I squeeze her gently.

"What sort of training do you think they'll do?" I ask. "One of the fundamentals mentioned 'stretches' which has me concerned."

Minnie huffs a little laugh.

"Nobody said change was easy. Maybe they meant stretching like before a marathon."

"My medieval mind went directly to stretching on the rack."

"You should join the modern world more often." Minnie pokes my chest. "How are you feeling about this?"

"Overwhelmed, mainly. There's a lot of responsibility coming my way if I accept the challenge. I'm terrified, certainly, but also strangely excited. Honestly, I'm not sure what it all means yet."

Minnie reaches her face up and kisses me, long and slow. When we surface, she holds my face in her two hands.

"If you choose it, you will be a thoughtful, responsible

fundamental, and I think it will be the making of you." She kisses me again quickly then stands. "I need to clear my head. I can say hello to Shannon at the river, like the fundamentals suggested."

"Do you want me to come?"

Minnie shakes her head but lessens the sting of rejection with a smile.

"Thanks for the offer, but I'd like to be alone. Don't wait up."

I nod and she slips on her shoes and walks out the front door. She still needs her space, and I can give it to her. Her exit feels better when we part on good terms. There is a lot to think about, and I don't begrudge her time to come to terms with the revelations of this evening.

Minnie climbs into bed after midnight, bringing with her the scents of wind and rain. When I wrap my arm around her waist, she curls into me, and there isn't a better feeling in the world.

In the morning, I wake so early that the sun hasn't lightened the sky yet. Memories of the previous night's revelations strike me hard and fast, and my eyes pop open with instant alertness. Will the earth elementals contact me today? What will I tell them?

I already know what I want. The siren call of the elemental plane sings in my heart, and Minnie's blessing cements my resolve. I will prepare myself, defeat Xenia, and become the earth fundamental. New horizons beckon, and it's all I can do not to leap out of bed in my fervor.

Instead, I gently roll out to avoid waking Minnie and slip on jeans and a shirt. My coat is still draped over the coffee table where I left it last night. When I close the door of my apartment, I'm careful to shut it quietly. Minnie was up late, and I don't want to disturb her slumber.

I jab the elevator button, eager to get downstairs. Although earth lauvan cling to the cement walls of my high-rise apartment, the network is stronger on the ground. If the elementals want to contact me, I will make it easy for them.

I have questions they need to answer, but I'm also keen to do what I can to defeat Xenia. She thwarts me at every turn, and my heart revels at the thought of getting the upper hand over her. She won't expect this turn of events, and I can't wait to take her down and free Liam and the others. The look on her face when she realizes our game will be priceless.

I stride with confidence out of the glass doors of my apartment and turn to the left to find a quiet bench. There is a brief respite from the rain, although the wooden bench is soggy from last night's storm. I siphon off the water by pulling blue strands toward the ground, then I sit and drop my hands into the waiting earth threads.

I don't seek out elementals this time. The fundamentals said they would send someone for me, and I don't want to grab the wrong elemental by accident. Instead, I push a few of my elemental strands into the network and wait like a fisherman with a baited line.

I sit for five minutes in the quiet calmness before dawn. A presence touches my strands, and then another. There is an irresistible sense of earth from them both, but the essence of each has a discernable, distinctive flavor. They pull me into the network, and I follow, unresisting.

"Novice Merry Lytton," the two presences intone. Since we are within the lauvan, and I have no ears to hear their words, their voices speak directly into my mind. "The fundamentals sent us to prepare you. What is your answer?"

"First," I say to them with my thoughts. "I have some questions. No, wait, first you need names that I can pronounce." I sit with my sense of each elemental for a moment, soaking in their essences. Names float to my mind. As soon as I conjure them from my subconscious, I know the names describe the elementals perfectly within the confines of English.

"You are Quake," I say to the one with dark brown strands the color of loamy soil.

"Quake," his low voice says. It holds a hint of glee.

"And you will be Tremor," I say to the auburn strands.

"If you insist, novice," the other elemental says in a higher pitched voice. She gives the elemental equivalent of a shrug.

"I do. Now, you say you were sent by the fundamentals, but you could be any rogue elemental and I wouldn't know the difference. How can you prove you're trustworthy?"

"We will summon Air," Tremor says with a hint of impatience. "But we are telling the truth."

Almost instantly, silver strands descend among us, bringing with them the undeniable roaring sensation of the air fundamental.

"These are the trusted elementals I sent you," Air says. "They will prepare you."

"I had to check," I say, a touch defensively. "They could have been anyone."

Air gives the equivalent of a nod that I sense through the silver threads that surround me, then the fundamental disappears. I turn my attention to the waiting earth elementals.

"About those questions. What exactly will I be doing as the earth fundamental? How can I do it from a human body? Will I have to plug into the network every night? Can I still live a human life at the same time?"

"Your presence as a fully committed fundamental will be

119

enough to start," Tremor says. "You may live your human life for now and fulfill your duties during short excursions into the threads each day. It will become clearer once we begin your training. You may refrain from committing to your fundamental role until the end of this session."

"That's fair. How long will this take? I didn't leave my wife a note saying where I'd gone." It still ignites a warm glow in my stomach to say the word "wife" after so many years.

"It will not take long, by human standards," Quake says. "Time is a strangely flexible thing. First, lie down on the ground. This will allow your body to fully immerse in earth threads. We will stretch you before continuing your training."

"About this stretching." Pain from a wound inflicted during battle is much different from knowingly walking into discomfort. That takes a different courage. "How much is it going to hurt?"

"We don't know," Quake says. His voice is curious. "We have no human bodies. It might be painful, or it might feel like nothing. It is necessary, however."

"Fine." I exit the lauvan and walk to a patch of grass next to a rhododendron bush. Hopefully, it is out of the way enough that no one will spy me lying on wet grass in the early morning. I lie down and wince as cold water seeps through the fabric of my jeans. My fingers grasp the nearest strands, and I descend into the network. "I'm here."

"Good," Tremor says. "We will begin."

The two elementals flit around my human strands that lie in the approximate shape of my body. I watch the process with interest and trepidation through my elemental strands from a short distance away. Their clusters of lauvan glow with distinctive shades of brown and they wriggle through my chocolate brown strands like worms burrowing in dirt. Little by little, my strands loosen from their configuration. A strange tugging grips me, and an uncomfortable sensation has me panicking.

"Wait, careful messing with my human threads. They're already loose as it is. I don't want them flying away on me."

"They will never do that," Quake reassures me. He burrows into my foot strands and emerges at my calf. "They will not leave you until you die."

"Good." That has been a worry of mine for a few centuries, that my loose lauvan would eventually float so far from me that I would lose them forever and perish.

Fear of Tremor and Quake's motives keeps me tense. The only reason I haven't ripped their strands away from my own is trust in the air fundamental's endorsement. Vulnerable is such a mild word for what I currently feel.

Time is difficult to judge in the featureless world of lauvan, but eventually Tremor and Quake emerge from my human strands.

"That is enough for today," Tremor says in a brisk tone. "Tomorrow, we will stretch you further. Today, let's begin your lessons. If you are to replace Xenia as the earth fundamental, you must understand the role you will play and the abilities you will have."

"Oh, I can't wait for that day," Quake says fervently. "It's a mess over here with Xenia gone. I still can't believe she left."

"She cannot be trusted as a fundamental," Tremor agrees. "She has no respect for balance. Dormancy is the only proper place for her."

"She deserves it," Quake says. He sniggers. "Can you imagine? She'll be tumbling pebbles instead of powering plate tectonics. What a fall from grace. And she probably won't be sentient enough to know how far she's fallen."

"There is no need to gloat," Tremor says. "But I do agree, the world will be a better place once Xenia is not a fundamental anymore."

"No pressure," I mutter. More loudly, I say, "You'd better show me around."

"Follow us," Tremor says, and she takes off through the lauvan network. Quake swiftly follows, and I chase them to catch up.

CHAPTER XV

We follow brown earth strands that spread across the land. Multitudes of clusters of every color flash past us. It's exhilarating to soar through this aspect of the elemental plane like this. It feels right, somehow.

At an expanse of blue lauvan that corresponds to the ocean in the physical world, Tremor glides below the heaving strands. I have never considered doing that, and it is with trepidation that I follow. I feel the urge to hold my breath, but there is no air and no need for it in this existence.

Earth strands follow the seafloor under a mass of shifting blue above us. There are colorful clusters down here that signify fish, invertebrate, and algal life. We travel farther and faster, until a great gathering of earth lauvan rises before us. I stop in amazement, and Quake circles back.

"It looks like the edge of a tectonic plate," I say. I take in the expanse of brown strands that run across our path as far as I can see. "I've only ever seen them on land before. I've never thought to look under the ocean."

To be fair, I only recently discovered the ability to travel in the lauvan network without relying on cables. There hasn't been much time lately to explore.

"This isn't our end destination," Quake says. "Come on."

Quake dives into the mass of brown. I follow uneasily. Instead of shadowing the huge cable that runs along the seafloor, Quake descends below it. Strands reach down, far into the Earth itself. Deeper and deeper we follow Tremor, until the flickering orange of fire lauvan lick the solid strands of earth.

"Are we under the Earth's crust?" I say in amazement.

"Indeed," Tremor says. "Here is the seat of your future

power. When you are at full strength, you will be able to adjust the very Earth itself to find the correct balance."

The strands shift slightly, and Quake huffs.

"That's why we need you," he says. "Xenia should be taking care of this. Instead, she's gallivanting in the physical world. The plates aren't moving as they should be, and it's causing tremendous snarls on our side and earthquakes on yours. Do you know what just happened there? An earthquake under the seafloor. Give it another couple of days, and the shaking will be large enough to create a tsunami. There's far too much tension that's not being released properly."

"There are even new seamounts beginning to form where they shouldn't be," Tremor adds. "The gases are already affecting sea life in the surrounding ocean. If the chaos increases any more, the effect on Earth's climate will be catastrophic. The earth fundamental's role is crucial."

The power offered to me is truly terrifying and awe-inspiring. To have the ability to control the motions of the plates themselves makes me shudder.

But I could do it. The lack of balance unnerves me as much as it does Tremor and Quake. I could fix that, and determination solidifies my fears into solid purpose. Being the earth fundamental is not about being worshiped, as much fun as Xenia seems to be having. Adulation by the masses is not something I have ever wanted, so that temptation holds no power over me. If balance is what is needed, I can do that. Xenia has dropped the ball, and it's up to me to pick it up.

A thought strikes me amid the shifting earth and flickering fire strands.

"You're training me to have power of the earth," I say slowly, forming my plan as I speak. "Is there a way to have control over what lies on top? Say, if I could affect the ground under a region, what could I do to the creatures above?"

"You can concentrate your power in an area for a time," Tremor says. "Although you will be weaker in other regions during it. That will give you the ability to loosen the threads of those above. For example, if a tree is diseased, you could change the threads under its roots to give it a chance to heal itself. Only if it were necessary to maintain the balance, of course."

"Of course," I say by rote.

"And you wouldn't be doing anything that fine-tuned," Quake says. "Think bigger picture. That's why you have elementals like us to do the little stuff."

"But I'm not the fundamental yet. We still have to defeat Xenia. Can you take me to the surface and show me how to change the threads in a small area?"

Tremor leads the way out from under the crust and back to the familiar strands of the city. Under a tree, she and Quake twist threads by spinning around with their own clusters until a pattern emerges. I memorize it, although I prefer to twist lauvan using my hands.

"Thank you," I say once the elementals have dismantled their demonstration. "We will continue tomorrow?"

"If you have decided," Tremor says. "Will you become our fundamental?"

My gut clenches at the decision, but it only takes a heartbeat for me to answer.

"Yes, I will."

"Then we will come tomorrow. Enter the threads and we will find you."

The elementals disappear, and I flow back to my body. It shakes from the bone-chilling cold of my damp clothing, and every muscle aches. Is the discomfort from Tremor and Quake stretching me? I suppose I should be thankful it wasn't agonizing, but when my entire body protests at rising from the ground, it's difficult to muster gratitude. Again, my mind wanders to Tremor and Quake's goals. Did they deliberately weaken me? Air wouldn't have sent them if they weren't entirely trustworthy, surely.

I do feel different, though. Perhaps the best descriptor is that I feel roomier, more expansive. It's an odd yet freeing sensation.

I shiver my way up the elevator. The sky is still dark, although the east is lighter under looming clouds threatening another rainstorm. Minnie is still in bed when I come in and strip off my soaked clothes. She murmurs sleepily, and I button my shirt while I kiss her forehead.

"Go back to sleep, love," I whisper. I'm curious what the river elemental told her, but there will be time to talk later. I don't want to disturb Minnie's sleep. "I have something I need to take care of."

By the time I reach Alejandro's house, the sky is as light as it will likely get. The clouds are pregnant with rain, and I glance at them as I walk down the path to the side door. It takes a full minute of knocking, but Alejandro finally opens the door. He looks disgruntled and his hair is tousled.

"Merlo?" he says. "What are you doing here so early?"

"I have an idea for Liam." I push into the house and Alejandro blinks his sleepiness away. He shuts the door and follows me to the round table.

"Did you find something at the spirit library?" he asks. "I was going to head there today to help look."

"Not as such." I consider Alejandro. His eyes are alert by now, and he looks awake enough to receive my news. "The air and fire fundamentals visited me last night. They want me to take over as earth fundamental."

Alejandro grips the back of a chair.

"What does that even mean?"

126

"I get to keep my human body and life." I run my hand absently along the edge of the round table. Even after pondering the revelation for much of the night, I still have a hard time getting the news to sink in. "Elementals are teaching me what I'll need to do. The details are fuzzy, I'll admit, but the real perk is that the fundamentals will help take away Xenia if I promise to become the earth fundamental."

Alejandro shakes his head slowly, his eyes on mine.

"And are you going to do it?"

"Yes," I say without hesitation. My mind is made up now. After seeing the raw forces at work and the consequences of Xenia's inaction, I am ready to take on the mantle. "This is a way to get rid of Xenia forever. I am willing to accept the charge."

Alejandro nods, and his eyes crinkle.

"You'll be a good fundamental. If you can learn to work with others."

"There's the rub. I'll do my best."

"Here's hoping they can teach an old dog some new tricks."

I laugh, and the tautness of the moment eases.

"The real reason I came over so early is because the elementals gave me an idea for Liam. They showed me how to fix an area of ground to loosen the lauvan of anything above. The application they showed me wasn't exactly what I wanted, but I think I can make it work with some trial and error."

Alejandro stands up straight.

"Good, because I can't find anything to help, and Liam hasn't changed. Chloe is staying strong, but I know it's scaring her. What do I need to do?"

"I'll go to the backyard, try it there where the lauvan are thick. You get Liam up. I shouldn't be more than a few minutes."

I let myself out the back while Alejandro knocks on Liam's

bedroom door. The scruffy dirt patches of summer have given way to mud and shaggy grass. I find a drier section under a tree and bury my hands in the matted vegetation. When my eyes close, my elemental strands travel into the earth network beneath my feet.

I take a good look at the surrounding strands, then I pull back to my body and get to work. With a twist here and a knot there, the same pattern emerges that I saw Tremor and Quake construct below the tree. By the time Alejandro leads an unresisting Liam out the door, I have created a circle two paces in diameter that will loosen knots.

"Lead him here." I point to the center of the circle. "The pattern is made for a tree, so if it doesn't work, I have a few tweaks to try."

Alejandro's face holds nothing but confidence in my abilities, which I appreciate. He gently pushes Liam through the grass and onto the spot I indicated. I stare at the knot on Liam's temple. It wiggles then stills.

"Not quite," I say. "Let me try something."

I bend and twist a few more strands into a new configuration. The knot on Liam's head wiggles some more, and a few strands escape their bonds. Heartened, I tie more knots. Liam's strands wiggle with greater force, then they slink apart as if the knot had never been. I whoop with joy, and Alejandro races forward to peer in Liam's face.

Liam blinks a few times.

"Alejandro?" he says in confusion. "What are we doing in the backyard?"

"It worked!" Alejandro slaps me on the back, laughing. I stand upright and grin broadly.

"Welcome back, Liam," I say. "What do you remember of the last few days?"

Liam rubs his head in thought.

"It's all really blurry," he says. "I haven't been going to work, have I? There was a lot of bad television. And is Chloe here? I remember her."

"Do you remember going to Xenia's construction site with me and Minnie?" I ask. Liam's face darkens.

"Yeah, I remember that. Xenia's a piece of work, isn't she? Everything is fuzzy after that, though. What happened?"

"She brainwashed you with lauvan. Minnie and I only escaped because we could see what was happening. I'm sorry I couldn't warn you in time. Xenia is taking over Vancouver, one worship session at a time. She's forcing her followers to build her a temple." I pick up Liam's hand to show him the dirt encrusted underneath his fingernails. "You were working there too."

"We told Chloe about Xenia's brainwashing powers," Alejandro tells him with a hint of guilt in his voice. "She followed you to the work site, and there wasn't anything else to do."

"Damn it," Liam mutters. He straightens his shoulders. "Thanks for looking out for her. I'm going to get an earful from my sister when she hears from Chloe, though."

"At least you have your mind again." I clap him on the shoulder. "Come into the house. Chloe will be glad to have you back, I'm sure."

Liam takes two steps toward the house, then his feet slow. I glance at his face, and his eyes are vacant once more. The knot at his temple has reformed, and I gape in surprise.

"It wasn't a permanent fix," I whisper. Alejandro glances back at us, then his eyes widen at Liam's return to his near-catatonic state.

"Can you do it in the apartment?" Alejandro asks with urgency. "We can't lose him again."

"I'll try."

I race ahead, leaving Alejandro to guide Liam inside. Chloe eats cereal at the round table with a glum look on her face.

"Hi, Merry," she says. "What are you doing here?"

"Trying to fix your uncle." I bend at an exterior wall and twist strands into the correct conformation. Chloe already knows about strange abilities. She'll have to suffer one more revelation.

Her eyes bore a hole in my back as I seemingly wave my hands in midair around the walls of the apartment. When I glance at her, her eyes are wide and staring at me.

"Do you have magic too?" she whispers. I huff a breath of laughter.

"You can call it that if you wish. Now, hush while I work."

Alejandro enters and leads Liam to the round table. Chloe stares at him with hopeful eyes. It takes me another few minutes to complete my pattern, but it grows easier with practice. I make the final adjustment with a flourish and turn to look at Liam.

He blinks the vacancy from his eyes, and Chloe throws herself at his neck.

"Chloe," he murmurs and rubs her shaking back.

"That was horrible," she sobs. "Don't do that again."

"I'll try not to." He looks at me. "Now, what?"

"If you want to stay yourself, you'll have to stick to the apartment. Until I figure out a way to make this permanent or defeat Xenia, this is the only place you are out of her control." I shrug helplessly. "I'll keep learning, but this is new to me, too."

"Thank you, Merry," he says. "I mean it. House arrest is far better than being trapped in my mind, at the mercy of a psychopath."

Chloe cries harder at this pronouncement, and Liam looks guilty.

My eyes flick to the microwave clock, and my stomach lurches.

"I have to get to work," I say. "Liam, think hard to see if there is anything useful we can glean from your experience, any insight into Xenia. Chloe, work on the Liszt. Don't get sloppy with the twelfth bar. I'll come back later, and I'll know if you haven't practiced."

Chloe sniffs and nods, her mind focusing on the new task. Liam grins at me and nods his thanks.

I hop into my little blue van parked on the road, energized and full of hope. I freed Liam from Xenia's clutches, albeit temporarily, using my new training as an earth fundamental. There is more knowledge where that came from, and I'm thrilled to learn. Everything is novel, and I love it that way.

The university looks bright and cheerful to my eyes despite the rain which has burst forth in torrential sheets that sweep across the roofs. I anticipate a good day at work, full of eager students and interesting lectures.

I pause at this thought. I haven't felt that way about my classes in a while. Part of my restlessness and malaise I attributed to my disinterest in teaching. Minnie even brought home those personality tests for that very reason. What changed?

My early morning lesson with Tremor and Quake springs to mind. Was Minnie right? Was a lack of purpose, an absence of ambition and drive, causing my dissatisfaction? Now that I am training to be the earth fundamental, my path is laid before me, clear and straight. I have never known such certainty about my future, and it's exhilarating.

I should let Minnie know. She'll be pleased that her advice paid off. Everyone loves being told they were right. I have a few minutes while I walk briskly to my classroom, so I pull my phone from my pocket.

131

"Good morning, sunshine," I say brightly when Minnie answers. It's a reference to our first date when she wore a brilliant yellow sundress.

"Good morning," Minnie says with a smile in her voice. "What's up?"

"It's a beautiful morning. I had a lesson with the elementals earlier, and I made progress with Liam. He's not cured completely, but as long as he doesn't leave his apartment, he's lucid."

"That's wonderful news." Minnie sounds genuinely happy for Liam, but there's an undercurrent of sadness lining her words. I wish I could see her strands.

"I wanted to let you know, I think you were right. This whole fundamental thing is giving a direction to my life that I never knew I needed. I feel great. Even teaching is palatable this morning."

"I'm glad to hear it." This time, the tone of sadness is more apparent. "You've decided to become the fundamental, after all?"

"Yes. Minnie, are you all right?"

"Yes, love. I'm truly happy for you." Her voice is perkier now, as if she's smiling or at least forcing a smile. "This is what you needed. And I only have one thing to say."

"Which is?"

"I told you so."

I laugh aloud.

"You deserved that." I climb the steps of my building. "I have to go, I'm late for class. I'll see you tonight."

I sign off and stride with brisk steps into my lecture room. My class is assembled and chatting among themselves. The wall clock tells me I'm two minutes late. A glance at my watcher in the corner earns me a disapproving headshake and a note on the clipboard.

132

She is close enough to reach one of her loose lauvan, so I give it a little tweak as I walk by. She sneezes three times in quick succession, and I smile to myself.

I stride to the front of the room and clap my hands, eager to start this day.

"Who's ready for a little Shakespeare?"

My classes end at lunch. After a quick sandwich from the campus deli, I breeze through the papers I have to mark and wonder why I always felt that it was a distasteful task. It's not that much work, and some of the essays even glow with brilliance. I write a large red checkmark with a flourish on the final paper then leap up and leave my office.

I should check on Liam. Perhaps the strands need tweaking. And I promised that violin lesson to Chloe. Yes, a visit will do nicely.

My blue electric van rolls silently to the curb down the block from Liam's suite. I walk with springy steps down the side path and knock exuberantly on their door. After a moment's wait, Chloe answers. Her dour face punctures my bubble.

"What's wrong?" I ask.

"It's Uncle Liam," she says in a mournful tone. "He's gone back to how he was before."

She steps aside to let me in. I stalk forward, and my eyes fall on Liam. He's on the couch watching television again, and his head doesn't turn to the door upon my entrance. I walk over to him and snap my fingers in his face. He doesn't flinch.

"Damn it," I mutter, my good mood ruined, but my resolve strengthening. Xenia's manipulations were so strong that the knots on Liam's temple reformed, despite my healing

133

configuration around the apartment. Terrible wounds are similar, and healing must occur over multiple days. Liam's knot must be like a mental injury. "I need to check my morning's work. Give me a minute."

I walk the perimeter of the apartment with Chloe's curious eyes on me the whole way. Near the bathroom, the strands' pattern has loosened significantly. When I knot them back into position, Liam twitches.

"It's working," Chloe whispers. "Keep going."

Heartened, I shuffle further around the room. The rest is unchanged except for a patch under the kitchen sink. When I adjust that, Liam blinks and stands.

"Was I back in my state?" he says with chagrin. "That didn't last long."

Chloe sniffs, and Liam walks over to give her a hug.

"I'm sorry I keep scaring you, kiddo," he says. "I hope this will be over soon. Bad timing for your visit, hey?"

Chloe shrugs.

"I've already seen the sights of Vancouver. They're probably lame the second time around."

Liam chuckles then turns to me.

"Now, what? Do you keep fixing the lauvan every time they mess up? What's the long-term strategy?"

"Long-term, we're defeating Xenia." I walk to the round table and sit. The other two join me. "Short-term, I'm not sure. I can certainly keep coming back, but there must be a better way. Let me contact the elementals I was working with this morning. They might have a better idea."

There are enough earth strands below my feet to enter the network from where I sit, so I reach under the table and draw a few lauvan into my lap. I close my eyes and send my conscious into the strands.

It doesn't take long before the familiar essences of Tremor

134

and Quake materialize before me.

"Are you ready for your next training session?" Tremor asks.

"Not quite. My friend is in trouble, and I want you to check my work. He was brainwashed by Xenia. I made the loosening pattern under him like you taught me this morning, and it worked, but only temporarily. Is there a way to make the change permanent and free him from Xenia's clutches?"

The two elementals flit around the circle of patterned earth strands, examining my work.

"It's tight," she says. "But she is the fundamental, after all."

"Not for long, hopefully," Quake says. He joins Tremor at Liam's lauvan. "The pattern you twisted is good—I like your modifications, that's the sort of innovative thinking we could use in a fundamental—but there isn't enough grounding here. Try a different location."

"In the mountains, you mean? Or near a cable?"

"Either will do," Tremor says. "Or dig deep into the Earth, draw on the power below."

"He's not ready for that yet," Quake protests. Tremor circles my strands in consideration.

"Perhaps not," she says. "But after a few more sessions with us, he might be. Take your friend somewhere more amenable and try it. With luck, you can remove the knot permanently."

"Thank you," I say. "I'll come back for my next lesson soon."

I enter my body again and gasp a breath. Alejandro must have arrived while I was with the elementals, for he stops in mid-sentence when I return. Chloe looks at me with a white face.

"That was creepy," she says. "What did you do?"

"I found some answers."

CHAPTER XVI

"Let's go to the cable in Stanley Park," I say to Alejandro. "We can find a quiet spot in the trees. This time of year, there aren't many people braving the rain."

Chloe looks doubtfully out the window, where fat droplets splatter against the glass.

"We're going out there?"

"You should probably stay here," says Alejandro. "Do your homework or something. We won't be long."

"No way." Chloe stands and grabs her coat. "You're not leaving me behind, not when it's my uncle, and there is magic being flung about. I'm coming."

Alejandro shrugs at me. I wave everyone toward the door.

"Better wear something warm. There's a storm brewing."

We traipse outside to my blue van which is getting pummeled by the driving rain. Alejandro leads a foggy-eyed Liam to the back door, and Chloe buckles him into the seat beside her. We take off in a hiss of tires on wet pavement. It's quiet for a minute, then Chloe leans forward and perches her elbows on the backs of our seats.

"So, Merry," she says. "You have magic. That's weird but cool. How did you get it? Did you go to magic boarding school?"

I chuckle.

"Not quite. My father was an elemental who possessed a human body for a time. I never knew him, but he passed on his abilities to me."

"Huh. These spirit things Alejandro was talking about. That's kind of creepy, possession."

"Yes, it is."

"Can you do it?"

"Yes, I can."

This gives her pause, but not for long.

"Is there a whole underground magic culture? Oh, are unicorns and dragons real? What about vampires?"

"You've been reading too many books." I share an amused glance with Alejandro. "No, for most of my life I thought I was the only one. I've never seen a dragon nor a unicorn, and although I suppose I can't say with complete certainty that vampires don't exist, I find it unlikely."

"Too bad. A dragon would be awesome." Chloe taps her fingers on my headrest then glances at Liam. "And you think you can fix Uncle Liam for good?"

"I'm going to try."

There is plenty of room in the parking lot on this cold, stormy afternoon. I pull into a free spot and Alejandro jumps out to buy a parking ticket while Chloe and I lead Liam into the wet. Chloe wrinkles her nose.

"How long will this take?"

"I have no idea." I give her an evil grin. "Get used to the rain, princess."

She sticks her tongue out at me but doesn't argue further. Alejandro returns, and we walk along a path lined with wood chips that smell of damp cedar.

A few paces into the woods, Liam stiffens. He turns around and takes a step in the opposite direction.

"Grab him," I say to Alejandro and take Liam's arm in my own hand. "Xenia must be calling. Quick, drag him to the cable."

Alejandro holds his other arm, and we frog-march Liam to our destination. I'm glad no one is out because we look horribly suspicious. Chloe runs ahead to scout for spectators. Liam fights us every inch of the way, and I'm grateful for Alejandro's sword practice of late, which has given us both

137

greater upper body strength. We need every ounce of it to muscle a writhing Liam forward.

Liam's movements grow more frenzied. Sweat breaks out on my brow, and Alejandro looks worried.

"He's getting worse," he pants. "I don't know how much longer we can hold him."

"The compulsion is strong," I gasp. Liam bucks unexpectedly, and I nearly lose my grip. "Stop, this is insane. I'll have to knock him out."

Before Chloe's outraged expression can release in a cry of dismay, my fingers tweak a few strands at Liam's forehead. His eyes roll into his head and he drops like a boneless fish to the ground.

"What did you do to him?" Chloe yells and rushes to her uncle's side. I put my hands on my knees and catch my breath.

"He's fine, Chloe. Just sleeping. We couldn't fight him anymore. All right, Alejandro, let's carry him the rest of the way."

We prop Liam on our shoulders with his head dangling and his feet dragging. A jogger runs past, confusion and suspicion on her face. I nod at the unconscious Liam.

"Don't tell his fiancée," I say to her. "It was a night to remember."

She looks affronted but less suspicious and gives us a wide berth as she passes.

Finally, the cable winks at me through the trees. I point to it, since it is invisible to the others, and Alejandro and I gasp our way closer. When we are within touching distance, I put up my hand, and Alejandro gratefully lowers Liam to the ground.

"Now what?" he wheezes. I wipe my forehead on my sleeve and regard the cable.

"Now, I get to work. Find some shelter. This will take a few minutes."

Chloe needs no further encouragement and scuttles under the relatively dry overhang of a large Douglas fir. Alejandro joins her, and they watch me as I twist and pull strands. I keep the pattern tight around Liam since I'm hoping this will cure him. He won't be living on this patch, that's for certain.

It takes ten minutes of careful knotting before I am satisfied with the initial phase. Chloe looks bored in the way only a modern adolescent can, and Alejandro has stopped trying to engage her attention and merely leans against the tree waiting for me to finish.

The pattern is set, but I need to power it. The lauvan cable glimmers beside me, beckoning with its endless strands twisting and writhing in a mesmerizing flow. I take a deep breath and plunge my hands into the mass.

My head is thrown back with the sensation. I'm usually prepared for this, despite its overwhelming pleasure verging on pain, but my recent stretching with Tremor and Quake must have changed me. I feel the flow of energy far more than I usually do. It fills every part of me, and I know that the preparation both allowed me to feel more and made me able to handle more.

It takes a long moment and extreme willpower to wrench myself from the sensation, school my features into a semblance of calm, and pluck the few strands I need from the cable. I weave them into my pattern, and the ring around Liam begins to glow hot with the warmth of a sun-kissed rock.

My eyes search for the knot at Liam's temple. It twitches, then the strands wiggle loose from their binding. When they flow free once more, I untangle the cable's strands and allow them to return to their source. With a quick massage around the circle, I release the knots in the earth strands then bend and touch Liam's lauvan, sending my intention into him.

"Wake up, Liam," I say softly. "Let's see if you're back with

139

us."

Chloe and Alejandro hurry over when Liam blinks his eyes. He looks confused, which is more hopeful than his usual vacant expression. When his eyes flicker to mine, I know he's back.

"Merry?" he says and sits up with a groan. "Where are we this time?"

"I needed a cable." I stand and hold out my hand to Liam. He takes it and pulls himself to his feet. "You're not in an enclosure this time. With any luck the fix will hold, and you'll be able to go where you like without fear of compulsion."

Liam closes his eyes and exhales a long sigh.

"Thank you, Merry."

I pat his shoulder.

"This is all conjecture. You might not be out of the woods yet, but it looks good so far."

"Stop leaving me," Chloe says with her hands on her hips. Her jaw juts out, but her bottom lip trembles slightly. Liam huffs a laugh.

"I don't want to, believe me. Merry says I might be cured."

"Good." Chloe looks at him for a moment, then she punches his shoulder and hugs him.

"It's horrible," Liam says to us over Chloe's head. "Being brainwashed like that. I was in a weird fog the whole time. The only time I felt clarity was when I got a call."

"What was that like?" I'm curious how the compulsion manifests.

"It wasn't words in my head," Liam says. Chloe detaches from Liam but tucks herself under his arm. "More like I knew what I had to do, and it was so important that it was done right away."

"This needs to stop," Alejandro says. His eyes are hard. "Merry, you should work on your fundamental abilities. We

140

need to release everyone from the brainwashing. Why don't you do it now? We can watch your body."

I look at Liam and Chloe, neither of whom look like they want to hang around under a dripping tree in a rainstorm while I converse with elementals. Alejandro is right, though. The sooner I am ready to take over my fundamental role, the sooner we can overthrow Xenia. I dig into my pocket and toss Liam the keys to my van.

"You two go home. Alejandro and I will find an alternate mode of transportation when I'm done." I glance at Alejandro, who grins back when he catches my meaning.

Liam and Chloe don't argue. Liam puts his arm around Chloe's shoulders and steers her toward the path. I look around for a dry spot under the tree.

"What do you do now?" Alejandro asks. I lie down and close my eyes.

"You're looking at it. Get comfortable. It will be dull for you."

The sounds of Alejandro shuffling against the tree trunk fade as my elemental lauvan flow into the earth network. Within moments, Tremor and Quake are at my side.

"Good, you're back," says Quake. His dark brown strands twitch. Is he excited? "There's something I want you to try."

"After stretching," Tremor says with a hint of reprove. "We must prepare him for his coming role."

"Yes, yes," Quake says. "I know. After stretching."

I stay still and watch my human lauvan submit to the ministrations of the two elementals. My apprehension is almost gone, but it's difficult to release all my fears of the elementals' motivations. Once, a lauvan snaps, and I recoil instinctively.

"Watch it," I say. "That's going to hurt when I get back to my body."

"Sorry," says Quake. "I pushed too hard. We're trying to stretch you as fast as we can, but your body can only handle so much at once. I'm walking a fine line."

"I'll fix it later. Just—take more care, please."

Tremor swoops in and out of my strands, pressing her own threads against mine in a practiced manner. Her movements are swifter and more streamlined this session. I feel a little ill at the thought that neither elemental has stretched a human-elemental hybrid before. It's doubtful either of them has been around long enough to have interacted with a half-elemental in this way. From what I understand, the last time elementals freely crossed between the worlds was long before I was born.

When both elementals leave my body's strands, Quake comes up to me.

"Now, for the fun part," he says eagerly. "I want to teach you how to animate earth."

"What do you mean?" I'm flummoxed. "Make it move around? I can do that already."

"This is different," Tremor says, her voice more composed than Quake's. "When you move earth, you pull threads to disturb it from its place. Animating earth gives it your own threads so that it can move on its own."

If I had eyes, they would be wide with interest.

"Do I give it shape? Is this a humanoid dirt pile walking around, doing my bidding?"

"If humanoid is the shape you prefer," Tremor says. "Although I suggest mud instead of dirt."

"Holds shape better," Quake says. "I've never seen one—obviously, I've never been to your world—but I've heard stories. Only the more powerful earth elementals could create them, back in the day. It's a simple procedure, but it takes some power behind it."

"I don't have that much power," I say, thinking of my battles

142

against elementals to date. "Xenia wipes the floor with me."

"Xenia is the earth fundamental," Quake says with exaggerated patience. "She is stronger than everyone. It's not a fair comparison. But, in relation to other elementals, you pack a punch. I think you'll have enough to do this. Are you up for trying?"

"Always." It's true. Trying anything new always excites me. My strands wiggle in their readiness. "What do I need to do?"

"It's best if you take your human form," Tremor says. "We will emerge from the cable and give you further directions."

The elementals drift toward the glowing cable nearby, and I slide into my body. I open my eyes with a gasp then sit up. Alejandro looks over at me.

"Done already?"

"No." I stand and brush fir needles off my clothes. My entire body aches from the stretching, and my leg cramps horribly from Quake's mistake. I shake it out gently. "I need to be in my body for this next part. There might be something to watch if you're lucky."

"Are you ready, novice?" Tremor says from the cable where she and Quake hover in their nebulous lauvan forms. Alejandro jumps in surprise.

"Are the elementals here?" he hisses. I wave at the cable, invisible to Alejandro.

"They're in the cable, here to give me instructions on how to animate earth. All right," I say to them. "Lay it on me. What do I do next?"

"Find a patch of mud," Tremor instructs. "Any patch of ground will do, you can pull out earth from under grass if needed."

"Mud?" I look around at the sodden grass between giant fir trees. Rain pelts down in a steady sideways sheet. "I can probably manage that."

Alejandro snorts behind me. I square my shoulders and step into the deluge. The rain immediately soaks my hair and runs down my hoodless coat.

"What now?" I shout, regretting my choice of rainwear. Quake disappears from the cable, then a deep brown glow outlines a circle on the ground. As I watch, fascinated, the outline twists and knots.

"Memorize the pattern," Tremor says. "It will disappear once Quake removes himself from the threads."

I nod absently. The pattern completes, pulses twice with light, then fades away. Strands unravel and flow freely once more. Quake reappears beside Tremor.

"Do that, but in whatever shape you want," Quake says. "Give it some legs to walk around on. You're the half-human, you ought to know what would be best."

I glance at Alejandro, who shrugs with a smile.

"What kind of mud monster will you make, Merlo?"

I grin, wipe the rain from my eyes, and face the mud once more. My knees drop to the ground—I'm already soaking, so I'm not concerned about a little mud—and my fingers reach for the earth strands that float lazily a handspan above the ground.

I twist strands together while I recall Quake's instructions. Slowly, the glowing silhouette of a man appears, like a chalk tracing of a victim on the pavement. When the pattern is complete, I sit on my heels and gaze at it critically.

"Now what?" I ask. "Say the magic words?"

"Now, you must place a thread of your own in the pattern," Quake says. "Use an elemental thread, not one of your human ones. Weave it into the pattern, then you can direct the animation however you wish with your intention."

"Sounds simple enough," I mutter. I look at my hand. It is difficult to tell which lauvan are human and which are elemental, but when I touch the strands, some are thinner than others. I carefully tug a strand free from my body.

"Are you sure I should be doing this?" I ask with trepidation. "This is a part of me I'm putting in something else. Do I get it back later?"

Quake gives the equivalent of a shrug from his cable perch.

"Probably. Let's try it."

"Easy for you to say." I take the loose strand and tuck it into the pattern. Quake's instructions left an empty slot which calls out to be filled, and I oblige. When the weaving is complete, the outline glows and there is a strange tugging at my center.

"That's it," Quake says. "It's working."

"Raise it up," Tremor says. "It is part of you, now, so take control."

I'm not certain how to do as Tremor instructs, so I send out my intention despite not touching the lauvan. The outline glows, starting from my tucked-in strand. Hardly daring to believe it, I pour forth more intention. With a sucking, squelching noise, the rough figure of a man pushes up from the ground, sits, then stands. Its features are formless, and it drips onto the already sodden ground. My head starts to pound, but I ignore it in light of the creature before me.

"What the hell is that?" Alejandro whistles in awe. "You've done a lot of weird stuff, Merlo, but this might be the weirdest."

"You did it," Quake says. There's a hint of paternal pride which makes me chuckle. "I've always wanted to see that. The stories are full of strange, physical-world feats that we can only listen to and wonder about."

I send out my intention to the mud monster. It raises a formless hand and mimes scratching its head. With no nails and hands made from soft mud, the motion only slicks off some muck from its head.

145

"It's a like golem," I say. "From Jewish folklore. Incredible. I wonder if the cultural memory of beings like this passed down from millennia ago."

I send my thoughts toward the golem. It stumps toward Alejandro on stiff legs, and he shuffles sideways with a look of restrained horror on his face. I laugh.

"Give me something for it to do," I tell him. His forehead creases in thought.

"Can it be useful?" he says. "In a fight, I mean?"

"Ever the strategist." I tilt my head and consider the motionless golem. With a flash of my thought, the golem bends and picks up a fallen branch. With a few steps, it nears the tree. I'm getting the hang of moving the golem around, and when it swings the branch at the trunk, it is with deadly swiftness. The rotten branch crumbles against the bark, then the golem is motionless once more. I press a hand to my roiling stomach.

"Imagine a whole army of these," Alejandro says in awe. "They can't be hurt since they're made of mud and aren't even real. But you can make them do whatever you want."

My vision tunnels, and I drop onto my hands and knees until the lightheadedness recedes.

"I don't know about an army," I say weakly. "The effort takes a toll."

"Interesting," Quake says. "I haven't heard that part of the tale before. That detail doesn't make for a riveting story, that's for certain."

I stagger to my feet and walk toward the golem.

"Perhaps." My fingers tug my strand out of its weaving and tuck it back into my center. The golem dissolves into a pile of muck at my feet, and I jump back in distaste before my already wet shoes are covered in a layer of filth. "It's an interesting trick to have in my back pocket, but I won't make it my first line of defense."

Tremor nods.

"You will have many more options once you are the fundamental," she says. "But that is enough for now. Let your body recover from the stretching and contact us tomorrow."

She and Quake melt into the cable. I sigh and stretch my arms above my head.

"Are they gone?" Alejandro peers at the cable that he can't see. When I nod, he exhales. "You have a strange life, Merlo."

"Says the man who keeps being reborn." My entire body aches, but it is almost in a pleasant way now that it is familiar. I know its purpose is to prepare me, and therefore the discomfort is a productive one. Taking real action to prepare for my role as fundamental fills me with satisfaction. It will allow me to take down Xenia and build a better world for Earth and the elemental plane alike. Quake and Tremor's anticipation for my ascension is rubbing off on me, and I can imagine taking my place at their side to govern the world of the elements.

A part of me is nervous at the thought, but the larger part is excited. I'm ready for this. Centuries of experience have led to this moment and prepared me for this role. I don't know how I lived for so long in my aimless ways.

Alejandro looks at the gray skies.

"How does an eagle feel about flying in a storm?" he asks. I chuckle.

"You're in charge. Just shake your tail feathers and push through."

Minnie is home when I arrive. She comes out of the kitchen licking a large wooden spoon, then her mouth hangs open at

147

the sight of me inside the front door.

"Did you go swimming?" Her eyes travel to my muddy knees and filthy shoes. "Do not come in here. Take everything off at the door."

I grin and start to shed clothes.

"As my lady commands."

Minnie crosses her arms and watches me, trying to hide her smile. I ham it up for her, happy for this little bit of normalcy in a relationship that has grown increasingly strained of late. She snorts. When I am fully undressed, she smacks my bottom with her spoon.

"Dinner's in ten minutes. Wash up."

I hop into the shower and am clean and dry in five minutes flat. I want to spend time with this newly affectionate Minnie. I have missed her.

She's at the stove, stirring sauce and checking pasta noodles for tenderness. I slide my hands around her waist and kiss her neck. She turns her head to maneuver her lips closer to mine, and I oblige her silent request.

"That's strange," she says when our lips part so she can stir her sauce again. "Check out our lauvan."

My arm lies across her stomach, directly over her center. To my surprise, my brown strands are wriggling up my arm as if fleeing, and Minnie's blue threads are equally averse to touching mine.

"What does it mean?" I ask, fascinated. My fingers push one of my retreating strands into her center. Minnie winces, and I desist. "Did you feel that?"

"Yes. It wasn't great." She curls her index finger around one of my strands. Her own avoid mine, and her touch on my lauvan isn't as pleasurable as it usually is. A terrible thought pounces on me.

"Do you think this has something to do with my preparations

for becoming the earth fundamental? The elementals are stretching me to better contain the power."

"Water is my element, after all," Minnie says. "I am the daughter of—of a water elemental. Maybe I'm reacting to your changes. Does this mean we're incompatible?"

I squeeze her waist, angry at the thought.

"Never," I whisper in her ear. "You'll always be mine. I'll always be yours."

"Denial isn't an attractive trait," she snaps, her lauvan tight, then they droop. She sighs. "Sorry, I didn't mean to bite your head off. The personality came out again."

"I understand." I don't, not really, but I want to support her. Every time she reacts like this to something I say, I feel her slipping away. It frightens me, and our hostile lauvan are another straw on the proverbial camel's back. I'm nervous for the day the camel breaks.

Minnie is quiet and contemplative. We eat dinner without much conversation, but I don't want to leave our discussion so open-ended. After we bring the dishes to the kitchen, I take her hips in my hands and draw her near.

"I don't care what our lauvan are doing," I whisper to her. "Most people can't see the blasted things, anyway. Body language is much more powerful."

Minnie smiles, but her eyes are sad.

"Then talk to me," she says and wraps her fingers in my hair. I pick her up and carry her to the bedroom. Our kisses are slow and exploratory at first, but Minnie's lips soon press against mine with a desperate force. I attribute it to passion until the wetness on her cheeks rubs against my own.

"Are you crying?" I ask in bewilderment. "What's wrong?"

Minnie shakes her head and grips my face in her hands.

"Don't stop," she whispers. "Please. I need you. I need to be close to you."

I don't understand what she is upset about, but I would never deny Minnie anything. My hand strokes her leg, but when I glance at it, her strands skitter away from mine.

This hurts more than I expect it to. One of the pleasures of intimacy is lauvan connecting between the two parties. Without it, physical contact feels lacking.

The cord of strands that connects us, chocolate brown and midnight blue together, is still intact and strong, although there are signs of fraying. Something splinters in my chest. I can't let Minnie drift away from me. Whatever this rift is, we can beat it. We have been together for too long to let something like this force us apart. I close my eyes to ignore the lauvan and Minnie's tears and lose myself in her embrace.

CHAPTER XVII

Dreaming

From my vantage on the cliff's edge, I watch a cluster of riders canter between trees. Although it's too far to see faces, I can imagine their grim expressions. After all, I stole their human sacrifice in the dead of night and whisked him away from their ceremony that was supposed to contact the so-called elemental spirits.

The sacrifice in question shifts at my side.

"Is it them?" he asks. His face twitches with nerves.

"Calm yourself, Drest," I say with feigned confidence. "They're a long way off yet, and they're on horse. We can lose them in rough terrain."

Despite my words, I lead Drest back to the main trail. We need what speed the beaten path can give us. The sea is still a day's walk away, and I don't know how far the nearest port is. I plan to board a ship to cross the sea that separates Eire and my homeland, and I expect Drest will join me. He was captured and enslaved from his home in northern Britain, after all.

We stride quickly through the woods. Drest gamely keeps up, although our pace exerts him. He needs more food than he has been fed of late, and our rapid pace hasn't allowed for much hunting. My meager supplies of bread are almost gone between the two of us.

"Can't they use another slave for their sacrifice?" Drest says in exasperation after an hour's march. "Not that I want someone else to die, but why all this effort to chase me? I'm nobody to them."

"You were prepared," I say absently, my ears always

151

listening to the road behind us. "They say there is only a short window of time when the spirits can be contacted. The correctly prepared person must be sacrificed at the right time. They hope they can capture you before the window closes."

"Wonderful," he mutters. "I wonder how far the sea is from here."

Craggy cliffs rise on either side of the path, and I slow in hesitation. The trail follows a narrow gorge with sheer rocky walls teetering overhead. If we start down that path and aren't fast enough, the riders will overtake us easily. If we attempt to go around, we could waste precious days climbing over dangerous boulders only to find our pursuers waiting for us on the other side.

"We'll have to risk the road," I say. "Step lively."

Although I have only seen eighteen summers, something about my bearing makes Drest accept my leadership. Perhaps I rose in his estimation after my rescue of him. Whatever the case, he follows me without question into the gorge.

It's not long after we enter that the unmistakable sound of hoofbeats on packed earth causes my gut to clench. Drest stiffens.

"They're here," he hisses, panicked. "What do we do?"

"Run."

Drest takes off without a backward glance. I look around frantically, wondering what I can use to slow our pursuers. There are mountains all around. How far do my abilities stretch? Could I move mountains if sufficiently motivated?

The prospect of death is highly motivating. If I make the slope fall onto the path, the riders will have no way to reach us. I grasp a handful of earth strands and pull to see what will happen. Loose pebbles lift in a spray of gravel and shower me in dirt. I curse and run after Drest. I should have known I couldn't topple a mountain. That is too large a feat, even for me.

As I run, I scan the cliff for ideas. Loose scree covers the left side, and dangling brown lauvan give me an idea. I gather them in my hands, and once I am clear, I pull.

A few pebbles jostle then tumble onto their fellows. Those wiggle loose, and suddenly the whole hillside is sliding in a dusty roar behind me. I spring clear and watch in amazement as the gorge fills with debris.

I may not haul mountains around with my abilities, but I can tug at a crucial point to achieve my goals.

"Are you all right?" Drest hauls me forward and gapes at the dusty mess that settles across the path. "What happened? There's no way they are getting through that."

"Good." I pat him on the back and turn him around. "Then we will have time to reach the sea. Thank the goddess for freak accidents."

CHAPTER XVIII

Today's classes don't start until mid-morning, but I have a few things to do first. I descend in the elevator to the grounds below my apartment and place a blanket down before I lie on the damp grass. Tremor and Quake are waiting for me when I enter the network.

"Just a quick stretch this morning," I say. "And I can come back later for a lesson. I want to stop by Xenia's temple before work to check her progress."

"That's fine," Tremor says. "The stretching is the crucial part. You can learn when you are the fundamental, but you can't become the fundamental until you are stretched enough to receive the power."

"How much more do I have to do?" I already feel roomier than I did before, and my muscles still ache from yesterday's session.

"We'll see what we get done today. It might be enough."

"Or enough that you would survive the transition," Quake adds. "More would make it smoother."

I shudder.

"Carry on. I plan to survive."

Tremor and Quake get to work, and I watch the now-familiar process while my mind wanders. When they complete their task, I ask the question that formed while they worked.

"What I did to my friend Liam, the one with the knot at his temple, could I do that with more than one person at a time?"

"In theory," Tremor says. "You would have to create a large pattern around the group. It would take a fair bit of power, too."

"He's getting there, though," Quake says. "With the stretching we're doing, his own latent power is expanding to fill the space. He has more than ever before."

"Not enough to send Xenia to the elemental realm by himself, of course," Tremor says in a reproving tone.

"Of course," I say in reassurance. More power is interesting, though. Have I been contained in my human form with limited abilities? It's a thought-provoking notion. "But the pattern is possible, in theory. Good. Now, I need to go, but I'll return soon for another lesson."

We say our farewells, and I return to my body. I'm grateful it hasn't started raining since I'm chilled as it is. I leap to my feet, energized by my talk with the elementals, then my body screams in protest. The leftover ache from this morning has intensified, and it takes everything I have not to grimace as I hobble down the stairs to the underground parking. I hope this stretching is helping me, not simply weakening my defenses so Xenia can swoop in for the kill. When I reach my van, I drop into the driver's seat with a sigh of relief.

Ten minutes later, I pull over to the curb a half-block from the construction site. There's no need to advertise my presence. To be extra cautious, I twist my lauvan into the disguise of a middle-aged man with an umbrella. I stroll with unhurried steps toward the site, which draws me closer with the noise of hammers and machinery.

At the street, I stop to survey the scene. My eyes widen at the sheer size of the temple. It's almost complete and juts out from the cliff. It's four floors high at least, and the pillars that hold up the roof are simultaneously welcoming and forbidding. Parts of it look like they have grown organically from the bedrock of the cliff, but a large section extends from the rock to form a sprawling edifice. An opening in the ceiling hints at an inner courtyard, but the ground is too far below that the bottom is swathed in darkness.

Workers swarm the building like ants on an anthill. Rickety

155

scaffolding holds their numbers, although some climb nimbly on the roof with apparent disregard for their safety. Many hold chisels and chip away at the mighty stones that make up the walls of the structure, and others slap on mortar to smooth out cracks. The area on the ground before the main entrance is being reworked as well, with impressively large paving stones in concentric rings that lead the eye toward the main door. A mosaic of a mountain is placed in the center of the middle ring.

The number of workers is truly daunting, and I shiver at the telltale lauvan knot at every temple. Xenia controls the minds of so many. Even the skeptical, elderly dog walker I met the other day wields a bucket of mortar while he perches on the top floor of the scaffolding.

My mouth is slightly agape as I survey the scene, but it snaps shut at a familiar voice.

"Have you come to marvel at my glorious temple, Merry?"

I turn my head so fast that my neck clicks. Xenia stands beside me, wearing a toned-down version of her full ceremonial garb from earlier. The headdress is a simpler one rimmed with shells and adorned with red cardinal feathers. She looks at the construction with a smug smile, then slowly turns her head to look at me.

There's no point maintaining my disguise if she knows who I am, so I release my strands and revert to my usual form.

"How did you know?" I ask.

"I've been expecting you. And I'm the earth fundamental. I can tell the difference between all shades of brown." She waves at my center. "Yours are distinctive enough, and a closer look reveals the two different sizes of threads."

What do I say to her? I hoped to avoid meeting Xenia, but now that we are face to face, is there something I want to say? Xenia beats me to it.

"What do you think of my temple?"

I pretend to look the building over.

"It's a touch ostentatious and heavy-handed."

Xenia smiles.

"Good. That's what I was aiming for. Humans respond well to overblown, I've found. The bigger and grander I can make this, the more authority I'll have. Soon, the entire city will bow at my feet."

"Why do you need this?" I wave at the temple. "All you have to do is manipulate their minds, and they're yours. You could walk around in rags, and with a twist of your fingers, everyone you meet would kneel before you."

"A scintillating thought, for certain. I admit, the pomp and ceremony appeal to me. I want to be worshiped the right way, a throwback to the elementals of the past. I want to be surrounded by earth, in a setting created by my toiling, devoted servants, raised up and adored by the multitudes. Why not? I can."

What can I say to that? Xenia clearly has her mind set on her vision, and it's so preposterous that there is no reasoning with her. The only thing I could say is that the other fundamentals plan to replace her with me, but I'm not stupid enough to warn her of that. The instant she realizes that truth is the moment I die by her hand.

Why am I still alive now that she's found me? Certainly, none of her followers would stop her from murdering me. They are entirely under her influence. I have no answer, so I risk asking.

"Why are we talking?"

"What, instead of me killing you?" Xenia laughs heartily. "What, my dear Merry, would be the point? You are an insect I could squash under my shoe at any moment with a delightful crunching noise. You pose no threat to me. Now that I have perfected mind control, I have an army at my disposal. You

157

might have defeated my elemental followers a few weeks ago, but that was in the past. Every day, I learn more and more about my new abilities. It's exhilarating. With this human body and my fundamental powers, only my imagination limits me, and I'm quickly pushing the boundaries of that. Look."

Xenia snaps her fingers—more for show than true effect—and every single follower working at the site stops what they are doing. With another snap, they all drop their tools and begin to kick their legs into the air in a cruel mockery of the can-can. Xenia chuckles.

"March was an admirer of forties-era musicals, and her memories gave me the idea. Amusing, isn't it? Now, imagine if I told them to attack you. You would fight them off, no doubt, although your human weakness would make you avoid hurting the innocent people behind the compulsion. But even if you buckled down and fought them off properly, how long could you last? How many dozens would it take?" Xenia smiles again, smugness leaching out of her pores. "I have more."

A cold shudder crawls down my back, although I do my best to hide it. It's a fruitless endeavor because Xenia can see my twitching lauvan as well as I can. I managed to save Liam from her control, but how can I scale that to hundreds?

"This temple is only the start," Xenia says. "A proof of concept if you will. I want worship centers all over Earth. It was laughably easy to convert these people, and more will come. Think of what a whole country's worth of worshipers would give me, or a whole planet's worth. I want to be bigger than Jesus, Allah, Buddha, all these higher beings that humans venerate. I want to rule them all."

"What do you really get from it, Xenia?" I still don't understand. Is this all for an ego boost, so she can be served fruit on golden platters by adoring servants? She doesn't need

158

to conquer the globe for that.

Xenia stares at me for a long moment.

"Perhaps a demonstration," she murmurs. "I forget how limited your mind is. Living among the humans for so long has narrowed your outlook."

She raises her arms.

"My people," she shouts. Her voice, although not deafening, is loud enough to make all the workers stop immediately and turn her way. "You have worked long and hard. Receive my blessing and bow before me!"

As one, her followers genuflect deeply. There is silence before Xenia speaks again. Her voice rings out clearly.

"My people, you are the followers of Xenia, daughter of Coatlicue. You have been chosen to carry out her blessed work. She is beneficent, and you are her chosen people. Fulfill your destiny, and you will be rewarded."

Strands float upward from every worker until the air above them is thick with a rainbow cloud of lauvan. It flows toward Xenia like a glimmering river and surrounds her in a flowing cape. She lifts her head to the sky to receive the strands, her face ecstatic. The strands swirl around her, then all at once turn to chestnut brown.

My mouth drops at the sight. Xenia pulses with power, the energy of all her followers that she has made into her own. I feel very small. My recent stretching with the earth elementals is laughably minor. Defeating Xenia, while never a guarantee, had felt more manageable of late. Now, it's a daunting, near hopeless proposition.

Xenia shivers with a blissful smile on her face, then she waves her hand. All her followers rise and continue their tasks as if they had never been interrupted. Xenia turns to me.

"You can't imagine how invigorating it is to have humans worship you," she says. "Their lauvan flowing to me, surrounding me, bolstering my own. It's intoxicating."

There is a commotion on the ground. An elderly man, too frail-looking to be laboring at the temple, has collapsed. Another follower checks his pulse then shakes his head at his fellows. Together, they lift the old man's body and carry it into the temple. A bitter taste coats my mouth as I watch the dead man disappear through the massive doors like an offering to a giant stone monster.

"Some days I take too much, and the weak ones don't survive," Xenia says with nonchalance. "It's unfortunate to lose a worshiper, but there are plenty more. Humans are so numerous, and they can breed without the constant struggle to maintain balance. At least, they don't seem to care about it." She laughs lightly. "It's one thing the mortals and I have in common."

Her eyes glaze over, and I peer into them in confusion. Her hand snakes out and grasps my forearm with a pincer grip hard enough to leave bruises. I rip backward from instinct, but Xenia holds on like a leech.

"Merry," she whispers. There is something about the way she says my name that makes me pause. Xenia blinks away the glazed look. "Merry, it's March."

My mouth gapes open. Is March truly still in there, fighting to escape her bonds?

"Stop toying with me, Xenia," I say hoarsely.

"Shut up, Merry," she hisses. "I don't have long. Xenia is too powerful. But I'm still here, fighting. Free me, Merry. There's a book in the library. It might help. It's called *Call of the S*—"

Her eyes lose focus, and I peel the suddenly loose fingers off my arm. A moment later, Xenia is back and acting as if she never left.

"It's too bad you didn't join me, Merry. We could have had

such fun ruling the world together. Instead, I will become the most powerful being on the planet, and you will be lost to obscurity. If you act against me, you won't stand a chance, not with armies of humans behind me."

"I won't let you get away with this," I say.

It's weak, but I can't leave her words unchecked. The dead man, starved of his lauvan and worked beyond his capabilities, passes in front of my mind's eye. Xenia laughs.

"Whatever power I had as a simple fundamental is nothing compared to the power coursing through my body now. It's dazzling." She smiles and wiggles her fingers in a mocking wave. "Goodbye, Merry. Enjoy your insignificance."

Xenia walks away. I clench my fists, enraged but unable to do anything about it. March's brief appearance is heartening and her clue to the library worth pursuing, but Xenia's display of power is daunting. How can I hope to defeat her? If she truly is collecting more power, will the other fundamentals stand a chance against her, since they are not being worshiped?

I run to my van, eager to escape from Xenia's temple of doom and arrive at my next class on time. Before I pull into traffic, I text Wayne and Anna. They have been diligent at searching the spirit library. Perhaps they can make sense of March's partial message.

Look for a book called Call of the S—something. March contacted me briefly from Xenia's stranglehold. She thought it might help free her.

I skid into class on time and proceed to enlighten my students about Renaissance literature under the watchful eye of my probation officer. Three long hours later, I leap out of the lecture room and dart between students in the hall to reach Wayne's office.

He types grades into his computer, although a stack of books with titles that belong in the spirit library stand in a pile on his desk. He turns when he hears my entrance, and his eyes are concerned.

"What's the matter, Merry? How did you hear from March?"

"I saw Xenia this morning." I clutch the doorway to steady myself from my exertions. "She recognized me at the temple site, even through my disguise. She didn't bother annihilating me—apparently, I'm no more than dirt on her shoe, threat-wise—but she did enjoy a good gloat. It's a weakness of hers, I'm discovering."

"But not really one we can take advantage of."

"I haven't thought of a way yet," I concede. "But for a brief time, March took control of the body. She said she's still fighting, and she mentioned half of the title before Xenia came back. It's worth looking into. If we can bolster March's fight within the body, she can help us from the inside when we take on Xenia."

"Literally, from the inside." Wayne grins briefly then sobers. "I couldn't check the library this morning, but Anna's been there for a few hours. Hopefully, March's cryptic message meant more to her than it did to me."

"After Xenia took back control of the body—she didn't seem to notice March's appearance—she demonstrated how she gains power. She's collecting lauvan from her followers and using it to increase her own powers." I glance out the window, remembering the flow of strands toward Xenia and the surge of power that followed. "It's frightening. If we don't stop her soon, I don't know if we ever will, even with the combined might of the other fundamentals."

"You don't know how powerful they are," Wayne says reasonably. "Three against one? Xenia would have to triple her strength to beat that. And the elements seem to be stronger together, so that will help."

"I hope you're right, but it sounds like we need to weaken

Xenia before the fundamentals can whisk her away."

"It explains why she's getting worshipers, though. I did wonder why she would bother."

"I had it pegged for an ego boost."

Wayne snorts.

"You would."

Anna appears in the doorway, breathless. She glances at me quickly and nods.

"Good, you're here too, Merry. I found March's book."

"*Call of the* something?" I stand up straight and look at her hand, which clutches a leather-bound tome the reddish color of arbutus bark. "Excellent. Did you figure out what she meant?"

"I think so." Anna opens the book to a page marked by an old receipt then runs her finger down the words. "The book is *Call of the Spirit*, and it's a manual for deeper spiritual connection with nature. Most of it seems like fluff, but there is one section that talks about possession. If the possessed person touches a certain gemstone, it will weaken the spirit's hold on the body. We'll need to spill Xenia's blood at some point after she touches it for the spell to have full effect, though."

"We'll cross that bridge when we come to it," I say. "So, we need to plant an amulet on Xenia?"

"A prepared one." Anna pulls a ring from her pocket. "It won't take long to prepare, but I wanted to do it with you so you can tell us if it's working." She wiggles her fingers. "With the lauvan, you know."

"Too bad I didn't have it earlier," I say with regret. "I was right next to her a few hours ago. I've done enough pickpocketing in my life to make a planting a ring in her pocket a simple matter."

Anna raises an eyebrow then shakes her head.

"Xenia won't let you get that close again, I'll bet. No, it will

163

have to be me."

"What?" Wayne jumps to the edge of his office chair. His brow contracts.

"Me," Anna says again. "I can spin a tale about wanting to be part of the spirit world again, March was my friend, et cetera. I'm a good liar. Aren't I?" She looks at me with expectation. I nod in resignation.

"It's true. Your lauvan scarcely give you away."

"You can't get that close." Wayne wiggles with agitation. "What if she brainwashes you?"

"I have news on that front, too," Anna says.

"You found something?" Now Wayne looks excited instead of concerned.

"I did. It was a productive morning." She hands Wayne an open book, this one with a green cover, and turns to me. "There is a spell of protection to ward off persuasion. I'm convinced that it will help against the brainwashing."

"But it's for persuasion by people and lesser spirits." Wayne looks dejected again while he scans the page. "Xenia is so strong, what use would this spell be? It would need a lot of power behind it to compete with her."

"I've been working on that," I say. "Leave it to me."

Wayne nods slowly, but his eyes drift to Anna.

"I still don't like it," he says. "There are too many things to go wrong. We're trusting in these books, which are not exactly magic manuals. This one with the spell is an anthropology textbook. I don't like you walking into the lions' den, Anna."

Anna puts her book on the table with the ring on top then takes Wayne's hand.

"We're all in danger," she says. "Everyone in the city. I don't want to be brainwashed, I promise you. But there's a good chance that I will be safe, and a better chance that I can help. If nothing works and I'm stuck doing manual labor for

164

the psychopath, then I guess I'm getting my hands dirty until the rest of you save the day. But if we don't try to stop her, then we're only delaying the inevitable."

"And we do have a plan to get rid of Xenia," I say in reassurance. "This will make it far easier, I hope."

Wayne sighs and squeezes Anna's hand.

"I guess so," he says. "But I don't have to like it."

Anna smiles and kisses him on the forehead.

"I don't like it either," she says. "But that's okay. Sometimes things have to get done."

I take the ring off the book and hold it out.

"Where's the spell, Anna? Let's get this show on the road."

Anna opens the book to her makeshift bookmark and points at the spot. I read the instructions.

"For demon possession? Close enough. Xenia is as tenacious and infuriating as the devil himself. Here we go."

I recite the Latin words and twist the ring counterclockwise. Immediately, strands from my body flow toward the ring, human and elemental alike. They wrap around the small band of metal and braid themselves in a circle until I complete the recitation, then they slow and swirl gently around the ring.

"It's done," I announce. "And hopefully it is stronger because my elemental strands went with it too. Now, what about the brainwashing spell?"

CHAPTER XIX

I pull over to the curb out of sight of the new temple, and Anna takes a deep breath.

"You okay?" Wayne asks from the back seat and puts a hand on her shoulder. Anna reaches up and touches it.

"Yeah, I'm good. Just nervous."

"Rightfully so," I say. "But don't let nerves get in the way of your task. You can do this, Anna. You're an excellent actress. Xenia won't know what hit her."

Anna nods with a small smile on her face at my compliment. She pulls out her phone and dials a number. Wayne's phone rings a moment later.

"Put yourself on mute," Anna says when Wayne answers. "Then you can hear everything that's said."

Wayne squeezes her shoulder, then Anna opens the door.

"Good luck," I say. I wink at her when she looks at me. "You won't need it."

Anna smiles wanly then walks down the sidewalk to the temple. Wayne fidgets when she's out of sight.

"Let's get a better look," he says. "I can't just sit in this van, thinking about it."

"All right. But stay hidden. Let Anna play her role."

Wayne barely lets me finish my sentence before he's out of the van and striding down the pavement. I hop out, slam my door shut, and follow in his wake.

Wayne finds a laurel hedge in a neighbor's yard which protects us from the drizzling rain and rustles inside it. I glance at the empty driveway then wriggle in next to Wayne. He peers through the foliage for a better view.

"There she is," he hisses. He pulls out his phone and turns up the volume. The noise of renovations crackles through the tinny speakers, bangs and clangs that pierce my ears. I look through the hedge to where Anna's green shirt is easily visible. She walks across the pavers in front of the main door, confident and bold.

"Where is Xenia?" Anna's voice out of the phone startles me. Wayne jumps and clutches the device tighter. A more distant voice answers.

"Inside."

The renovation noises grow quiet, and Anna's footsteps on stone echo through the speakers. She must see Xenia, for the footsteps quicken then stop.

"Xenia, daughter of Coatlicue." Anna's voice is full of adoration. "I am finally in your presence."

I glance at Wayne quickly before looking back at the worksite where Anna is no longer in sight. Anna is an excellent actress and has fooled me on more than one occasion, but the awe in her voice feels genuine. I shake the unworthy thought from my head. Anna has proven herself again and again. I will not doubt her now.

No such concerns must pass through Wayne's mind, for he only stares at the phone with worry for Anna's well-being.

"Who are you?" Xenia's voice is clear through the phone. She must be close. "You are not an initiate yet, I see. Are you interested in becoming a devoted servant to your earth goddess?"

Xenia must see that Anna has no knot on her temple. I swallow. If Xenia tries to brainwash Anna right now, either Anna will fall under her compulsion or Xenia will see that her tricks have no effect on the other woman. Either way, trouble will come.

"I wish to be more than that," Anna says clearly. "I was March's most trusted confidante, her loyal advisor, and her companion in our search for the spirit world. Now that she has

167

finally found the answer to her prayers—her spirit traveler is the goddess Xenia, daughter of Coatlicue—I am delighted. She is now your vessel, and I wish to honor her through you. I am knowledgeable in the way of the spirits, and I am willing to serve you in ways that your other followers cannot."

Anna is convincing. Xenia must think so, too, for her next words are said in a genial tone.

"Ah, yes, I see you in her memories. Perhaps it would be good to have a trusted servant by my side. I will consider it."

"Thank you, my goddess." Anna's voice takes on a longing quality. "Please, may I embrace you? Seeing March's body before me, I am overwhelmed by memories, and I would love to hold her in my arms once more. If it is not too presumptuous."

"It will do no harm, I suppose. Yes, you may."

The phone makes a rustling sound as fabric presses against the microphone. Bingo. Anna must be using this opportunity to slip the ring in Xenia's pocket. When the rustling stops, Xenia speaks again.

"I am glad to have you by my side, but I must make you a devotee. Your obedience to me won't be as strong as the others, because I know you will need your wits about you to serve me best."

I freeze. Xenia plans to brainwash Anna. Wayne throws me an anguished glance.

"We have to get her out of there," he hisses. "Now."

"She has the spell on her," I say, but I know that she needs to leave immediately. Xenia will be able to tell if the spell doesn't work. I snatch my phone from my pocket and quickly dial Anna's number, then I reach over to Wayne's center and yank at Anna's strands that connect her to Wayne. I need to alert her however I can to get out of there fast. A buzzing sound notifies us that Anna's phone is vibrating from my call.

"I am already devoted," Anna says with remarkable composure, but her footsteps echo through the speaker.

"Still," Xenia says. "It is tidier. And then I can use your devotion to fuel my power." There is a moment's pause. "There. Wait, why did it not work?"

I yank on her strands again. Wayne backs out of the bush.

"I have to go down there," he says. I hold onto his arm.

"You don't even have the brainwashing protection. Do you want to end up like Liam?"

"March and I performed many experiments," Anna says. "Perhaps one of them affected your abilities?"

"Get out," Xenia snarls. "I will have no one around whom I cannot completely trust. Out!"

Pounding footsteps travel through the phone. I close my eyes in relief then snap them open again.

"Come on, Wayne. Let's get the van and get her out of there."

Once we're in, I squeal down the road. Wayne flings open the back door and Anna dives in, then I peel away from the temple. Anna breathes heavily, her eyes wide with adrenaline.

"I did it," she says finally. Wayne hugs her tightly and they shuffle into the back seat and put on seatbelts. I grin through the rearview mirror.

"Nicely done. And with your mind your own."

Anna shudders, and Wayne puts his arm around her shoulders.

"I've had enough messing with my mind. I don't want Xenia digging in there, too."

"It's time for a round table meeting," Wayne announces after

169

a few minutes of driving. "Xenia is out of control, and we finally have something hampering her. We need to act now. Head to Alejandro's place, Merry. I'll call the gang."

By the time we arrive at Alejandro and Liam's house, a few recognizable vehicles are parked outside. I stride with long steps to the side door with Wayne and Anna holding hands behind me.

Inside, Alejandro greets me.

"Come in. Is today the day we do something about Xenia? I hope so because I canceled work and my date in preparation."

"So did I," Minnie says from the round table. "But my last client is always flaky, so I didn't feel too bad."

Jen and Cecil are at the table with Minnie, as well as Chloe and Liam. Liam looks a little vacant, and I walk over to him and sit.

"How are you doing, Liam?" I ask. My eyes rove over his temple, where a small snarl has formed.

"I'm in and out," he says. "Sometimes I understand what's going on, and other times it's all blank. I guess your fix wasn't permanent."

I clench my fists and stand.

"This has gone on long enough," I say. "Xenia must be stopped before the whole city is under her command. Anna, at great personal risk, planted an amulet on Xenia which will hopefully reduce her power. March is still inside her body and is fighting to be released, which will strain Xenia's defenses."

"What can we do?' Jen asks. "Even if Xenia is weakened, she still controls an army."

"I need you to give me a chance to take off the brainwashing of that army." I look around at my friends, all of whom share a look of grim determination. "If I prepare the ground around the temple like I did for Liam this morning, I can take away the compulsion, at least temporarily. With the human army out

170

of Xenia's control, and her weakened from March and the amulet, we have a good chance of taking her down."

"How can we help?" Alejandro says. He sits at the table and spreads his palms over the surface.

"I'll be focused on manipulating lauvan, so I won't be able to defend myself. We can try to be stealthy at first, but when Xenia figures out what I'm doing, she will throw her people at us. I need time to complete my task."

"We can do that." Cecil holds up a bag at his side. "I brought my tranquillizer gun."

"I'll borrow your sword, Merry," Alejandro says eagerly. I grin at him.

"Of course."

"We can do this." Jen stands. "We can all do this. Let's go."

"Hold on," I say. "I appreciate your drive, but we should prepare first. I want to get Liam in fighting form again and give you all protection against Xenia's compulsion. Anna proved this afternoon that it works. I don't need any of you joining Xenia's ranks today. I have no desire to fight my friends."

"I'd like to be useful again," Liam says with a grimace. "I hate feeling like a puppet."

"We'll get closer to the temple, and I'll fix you up at the cable," I say. "For now, let's get everyone protected, then I need to visit the elementals briefly."

I stand and wave Wayne forward. He nods.

"I'll show them how it's done."

He stands tall as I perform the spell of protection over him. Before long, the others are lined up behind him, and I place the protection on them one by one. Chloe comes last.

"You're staying here," I tell her. "There's no way you will be a part of this."

"I can't just sit in the apartment by myself," she wails. "What if you don't come back?"

I glance at Liam, but he is glazed over again and is indifferent to his niece's dismay. Minnie walks closer.

"We do need someone to stay in the van and coordinate our effort," she says. "Also, if anyone gets hurt, they will need to come back to the van and have someone look after them. Blankets and bandages, that sort of thing. Do you think you can handle that responsibility?"

Chloe's lip trembles, but she nods vigorously.

"Yeah, I can do that."

I raise my eyebrow at Minnie, who shrugs when Chloe turns to me. I don't want Chloe that close to the action, but I also don't want her to follow us because we left her at home.

"All right, I'd better protect you too, just in case."

Chloe gives me a trembling smile which I return. Once my spell is complete, I point her toward the closet.

"You'd better find those blankets. And a first aid kit."

She nods and rushes toward the closet. Minnie steps toward me and kisses my cheek. I smile until I notice my lauvan skittering away from hers. Why is it doing that, and how can we fix it?

"She'll be fine," Minnie says. "Are you going to talk to the elementals now?"

"Yes." I roll my shoulders and tilt my neck. "They're going to want to stretch me again. It's going to hurt."

"Is that wise, right before our task?" Minnie looks concerned. I brush away a stray lock of hair on her forehead.

"The more stretched I am, the better I can handle taking on the power of the fundamental. If today culminates in a showdown with Xenia, I need to be as prepared as I can be. Today might be the day that everything changes. I'd like to survive the transition."

Minnie swallows and looks down.

"Are you going outside to do it?" She slips her hand into

172

mine. "I'll walk you out."

"Thanks." To everyone else, I say, "Prepare yourselves. In a few minutes, we'll leave."

Minnie leads me outside then pulls me to the house wall. She presses me against it and kisses me passionately. I respond, eager as always to feel her body against mine, although there's a note of desperation to her hunger that I don't understand.

"I could have asked the rest of them to wait longer if you wanted to do this," I say breathlessly when we surface. To my surprise, Minnie has tears in her eyes. I wipe them away with my thumb. "What's wrong? Are you worried Xenia will beat us?"

"No."

"Are you concerned I won't survive the power transfer? Because the elementals think that it will be fine as long as I'm stretched."

Minnie shakes her head then kisses me again.

"I love you, Merlin," she says in Brythonic. "And I will always find you. Remember that."

She gives me a watery smile and steps away before I can question her words.

"Go on," she says with a return to briskness. "Get stretching. We want you primed and ready for your new role. The world is waiting."

She disappears inside. I would ponder her words further, but she's right. I need to plug into the network and stretch some more. Her moods are up and down these days, anyway. It could simply be her personality change coming out again.

I kneel on the wet grass in the driving rain and consider moving to a desert when I leave Vancouver. When my conscious enters the lauvan network, it's only a moment before Tremor and Quake find me.

"One more stretch," Quake says with glee in his voice.

"Then you're ready to take on the fundamental mantle. I'm so tired of the chaos. I bet the fire elementals don't mind—they're so chaotic naturally—but for an earth elemental, stability is key."

"Yes," Tremor says. "This is the last stretch. Take Xenia to an earth cable by the sea, then the water fundamental can come out of dormancy, and the three fundamentals can remove Xenia from the physical world. Then you can take on the role of earth fundamental."

"One thing at a time," I say. "Stretch me so I'm ready, but I still need to weaken Xenia first. There are a lot of steps to get to that point. And did you realize how powerful she's making herself with all these worshipers? It won't be an easy task."

"It will be pointless to take down Xenia until you are stretched." Tremor approaches my human lauvan, visible in the loose shape of a kneeling body. "You're correct. First things first."

The elementals get to work. I anticipate the aches in my body once I can feel it again. After a few minutes, they emerge from my strands and position themselves before me.

"You are ready," Tremor says. "It has been an honor to work with you, novice. The next time we meet, you will be one of us, but greater. We look forward to serving you."

"Get rid of Xenia for us," Quake says. "Return us to normal. We're counting on you."

The two elementals fade into the distance, and I return to my body. As I suspected, every muscle aches like I have battled a whole army by myself. With a few creaks and groans, I stand unsteadily on my feet then shuffle inside.

My friends are gathered at the door, waiting for me. They are dressed and armed with various weapons and grim looks. I'm proud to have them at my side.

"Xenia has been in control for too long," I say loudly. "Let's show her who really has the power around here."

The others cheer, and Alejandro opens the door for us to march outside.

Everyone piles in my tiny van. It definitely isn't legal, but no one bats an eye. I make sure that Chloe has a seatbelt, and the rest arrange themselves on the floor. Anna and Minnie share the front passenger's seat, neither of them looking happy about it. It isn't a far drive, so I'm not worried about being detained by the police. Officer Lee might help me out, but I doubt it.

When the lauvan cable comes into view, lying across the road above the temple site, I pull over. The sky darkens with approaching nightfall, unaided by gloomy storm clouds leaking rain in a steady pelt. Everyone exits the overcrowded van with relief. If there were any spectators, I'm certain we would remind them of a clown car. Casual passersby are far and few between in this neighborhood since Xenia's takeover. I gesture to Liam, who stumbles toward me, looking unsure about what he's doing here.

"Come on, Liam," I say in a friendly tone. "Let's fix you up."

Chloe wrings her hands and watches as I place Liam next to the cable and twist surrounding earth strands into the correct pattern. This is good practice for what I plan to do next, and I take mental notes about how I will expand this to encompass the entire temple site. I think it will work. I hope it will work.

"Is it done?" Chloe whispers. I ignore her to focus on my task.

"Give it time," Minnie says. "He'll get there."

"Done." I step back and look at Liam's face critically. "Liam? Are you with us?"

Liam blinks a few times, then his gaze sharpens.

"Thanks, Merry." He shakes his shoulders. "I hate that.

Okay, what are we doing now?"

"Making sure no one interrupts me. I'll pass you over to Alejandro for details. All right, everyone," I say to the group. They press around me, their hoods up against the driving rain. "I need to work in the four corners of the property. At that tree, where that lawn chair is, beside the garden shed, and at the fire hydrant." I point at each location, and the eyes of the others follow my finger. "I shouldn't need more than a couple of minutes at each spot. I hope to remain unnoticed for most of my work, so let's not travel in a cluster. Thoughts on strategy, Alejandro?"

"Wayne and Minnie, you're with Merry," Alejandro says. "Wayne for strength and Minnie to look out for lauvan. Jen, Anna, and Liam will take the left corner by the road. Look casual. Cecil and I will take the right corner. Watch for workers noticing Merry. At the first sign of trouble, text Minnie and go straight to them." He turns to Chloe. "Chloe, stay in the van and keep a sharp lookout. If one of us comes to the road with an injury you can get out and help, but not before. Okay?"

"Okay," she says quietly.

The soberness of Alejandro's speech and the reality of the scene must have dampened her natural inclination to argue. She turns and climbs into the van, where her face presses against the passenger's side window. I look at the others.

"Let's do this."

176

CHAPTER XX

I turn and survey the scene. Somehow, Xenia's workers finished the temple this afternoon. It's an ostentatious yet beautiful edifice entirely out of place with the neighboring architecture. Chiseled stone glistens wetly in the rain, and the whole structure is solid and unyielding. It's a mix of stone artifice and the appearance of being organically formed from the rock cliff behind it. I find it attractive, and I wonder how much of the appeal comes from my earth nature.

Crowds of people throng the front, all on their knees and swaying gently like seagrass in waves, oblivious to the raging weather. Xenia stands at the temple door, under cover from the rain. She holds up her arms to receive her worshipers' devotion.

And she receives it in spades. A torrent of multicolored lauvan flows toward her from the hundreds of people at her feet. She lifts her face to the sky and closes her eyes, basking in the sensation. There are so many strands surrounding her body that I can barely see her through the glow.

Minnie's mouth gapes open.

"She's charging up," she murmurs.

"That's why we have to stop the compulsion. It will remove her power source. Come on."

Minnie and Wayne follow me to the right corner where the fire hydrant is embedded in the pavement. They stand on either side of me as I bend to pull earth strands into position. This manipulation is on a grand scale, far larger than I have attempted before, but it should work. I yank great swaths of lauvan toward me and tie them in massive knots to mimic what I did with Liam.

Minnie gasps, and I whip my head toward Xenia.

"It happened so fast," she says with a hand over her mouth and her eyes horrified. "There was nothing we could have done."

Xenia's hands hover over a follower's chest as she kneels on the flagstones of the temple entryway. Lauvan stream from the dead man's body and surround Xenia's quivering form. The ecstatic glee on Xenia's face makes my stomach turn. Wayne's skin is tinged with green.

"Come on," I say, swallowing my revulsion for Xenia's callous disregard for human life. "This has gone far enough. We have to finish this. Xenia can't be allowed to kill anyone else. The sooner we stop her, the sooner the madness ends."

I jog to the next roadside corner. Jen, Anna, and Liam watch the crowd below for signs of notice, but nothing has changed yet. Xenia looks skyward, and her worshipers still face the ground.

It's not until I clamber down the embankment toward the lawn chair on the beach that Xenia's head lowers and whips toward me. I pause with indecision, then break into a scrambling run.

"She saw me," I throw over my shoulder. "Hurry!"

Wayne and Minnie need no further encouragement. Their steps pound behind me as we slip and stumble down the steep rubble slope to the water's edge.

I skid to a halt at the lawn chair. It stands on a gravel pad above a steep drop-off to the ocean. It's a lovely view of snow-capped mountains on the North Shore that I don't have time to fully appreciate in my current haste. It must be the neighbor's chair, and I wonder what they think of the current state of their community. Undoubtedly, the neighbor has joined the ranks of the worshipers behind me.

"Make it quick, Merry," Wayne calls out. He and Minnie stand shoulder to shoulder between me and the temple.

Shouting cascades toward us, and a glance affords me an arresting view of a horde of followers running down the hill, fury in each face. I curse and dig my hands into the lauvan.

Knot after knot, the pattern emerges. The shouting grows louder.

"What's the plan?" Jen gasps to Wayne. The others have arrived, with seconds to spare before the crowd descends.

"Run," I say, tying the final knot of my pattern.

We race to the last corner of the property. I plant my back against the garden shed and my friends array themselves in a semi-circle around me. Feverishly, I tie knots and twist strands.

The first of the followers reaches us. With a scream of rage, Minnie pulls water from the nearby ocean and dumps it on the closest group. Wayne and Cecil aim their tranquilizer guns to fire, and Alejandro wields my sword with accuracy, although he aims for non-lethal blows. Jen trades kicks and strikes that I recognize from her lessons with me. Anna holds a baseball bat and swings it around with a force that convinces me she was on a league in her youth.

I concentrate on my task, not easy to do with the commotion before me. I itch to join them, and it chafes that I perform fiddly work behind the scenes when I should be beside my friends in battle where I belong. They are holding their own, which I appreciate, because this last pattern is the crucial one in which I must weave in my own strand to tie it all together.

"Any time now, Merry!" Jen yells and smashes her hand into a man's nose. Minnie screams and sends a wave to swamp a group who has grabbed her by the feet. They splutter and cough a dozen paces away, but still Xenia's followers come, relentless like the rising tide.

"Merry!" Alejandro shouts. "We can't hold them for much longer!"

One twist, two twists, weave my strand in—I tie the last knot

179

and let my work go. My head whips up and surveys the scene.

Many of Xenia's followers stop what they are doing with expressions of great confusion on their faces. Cecil shoots a few more before he realizes that they have stopped attacking. Some are passed out on the dirt or lie moaning, clutching ankles or ribs.

"I need to go home," a woman whispers near Anna. "I don't know what's going on."

"Me too," an elderly man says.

They shuffle off, those who can walk, and wander toward the road. There are those, however, who do not look confused. Anger still boils on their faces. These are the true believers, those who didn't need their lauvan manipulated to follow Xenia.

"For Xenia, daughter of Coatlicue!" one shouts, and they surge forward through the retreating crowd. There aren't many left, but those that remain are fierce in their determination.

But this time, I can join in. I dig my hands into the earth lauvan and feel the raw power at my disposal. It's so much greater than I had before, thanks to my stretching, although according to Quake, it's only the tip of the iceberg. I'm nervous and excited to feel the real deal when this is all over. If we can defeat Xenia and her followers.

I yank strands and the ground trembles enough that the approaching horde stumbles to their knees. My friends and I surge forward, and it's easy to overwhelm the few faithful who are left on the ground. With a few swift blows to the head and some well-placed tranquilizer darts, the group is subdued.

Alejandro leans on the sword and whistles.

"That was too close, Merry," he says. "It reminds me of that ambush near the Severn, just after my father Uther died, remember?"

"Too well," I say. "But we made it. Is anyone badly hurt?"

"A few bruises, but we're okay," Jen says. She wipes her face free of the pelting rain. "It's not over yet, though. Xenia and her two air minions are still around."

"Two minions?" Alejandro chuckles. "That's nothing. We got the better of a dozen last month. We can handle two."

"Todd was with us then," Minnie says, but she doesn't look despairing. Instead, she looks thoughtful and a little sad, and I wonder what she's thinking. There's no time to discuss it, though, for the minions in question appear around the corner of the temple. The dark-skinned man with bleach-blond hair grins with a devilish glint to his eye, and a petite woman looks bored at what she must consider a minor task.

"Here we go," I say. "On your game, everyone. Two minions down, then it's only Xenia left. We can do this."

I don't know if we can, but we are the closest we have ever been. Alejandro's right. Last time, we faced over a dozen elementals, and now only two stand in front of us. That's one each for Minnie and me, and the rest of our friends can clean up the edges. I don't see how we can't prevail against them. Surely, after we defeat these two, Xenia will be stoppable. She may have the power of a fundamental, but after knocking down her minions and baiting Xenia close to the cable, we will contact the other fundamentals to wake Water. Then she won't stand a chance. The memory of Xenia receiving her followers' power floats across my mind, but I push it back. One battle at a time.

The driving rain suddenly pelts against our faces as the air minions channel the wind. Its strength takes my breath away, and all my energy is focused into making my feet walk one step in front of the other. With slow hands, I construct a lauvan barrier in front of me. Immediately, the wind dies.

"Get behind me," I shout to the others. Minnie steps beside me and creates her own wind barrier. The others range behind us and we push forward through the hurricane without issue.

The two minions glance at each other and split up to flank us. The howling winds die around our bubble, and Minnie and I lower our hands, ready for the next attack, but this time it's not from the air minions.

The others must have been whispering to each other, for with one motion Wayne and Alejandro each leap sideways toward the air minions. At the same time, Jen and Anna shoot tranquilizer darts at each elemental, and Cecil follows Wayne while Liam follows Alejandro.

"We're being shown up," I say to Minnie. She grins.

"Mine's the right one, slowpoke."

The air minions are not idle, but it must be difficult to concentrate with our lot barreling down on them. I follow Wayne and Liam and watch Wayne slam into the man, who crashes to the ground.

A blast of frigid air and piercing rain pushes Wayne off the elemental, but Liam is next, throwing punches with a snarl that shows his anger over his recent loss of control. The lauvan cable glimmers beyond them. While the minion is occupied, I reach for the lauvan at his feet and pull hard.

A cracking sound hits my ears, closely followed by a scream of pain. His leg must be broken. I don't waste my opportunity, and neither do the others. We converge on the minion, punching and pulling strands, until he passes out from the dart that punctured his arm during Anna's sharpshooting.

When I turn to survey the other battle, the others stand around a sodden figure crumpled on the ground. They are panting for breath but appear unharmed. I can't stop myself from pumping my fist in the air and giving a wordless shout of exultation. It was a battle well-fought, short though it might have been, and that we emerged victorious made it so much sweeter. We released followers from Xenia's mind control, subdued the devotees, and cut down the elementals. All that is left is Xenia herself, and without her wall of underlings to protect her, she is very alone indeed. With my friends behind me, my increased strength as an emerging fundamental, and my beloved Minnie at my side, I feel unstoppable.

I am ready to defeat my enemy and ascend to the role I was born to fill.

Wayne wipes mud and sweat off his face, which seems futile given the pelting rain coating every part of our bodies.

"What now, Merry?" he asks, his voice eager. He enjoys battles as much as I do. It must remind him of his past selves.

"Now, we find Xenia and take her down." I put my hand up. "Wait, first I need to contact the fundamentals. We need to wake up the water fundamental. With the three powerhouses behind us, you lot, and me, Xenia has no chance."

The others cheer and gather to strategize, but Minnie grows pale. Her hair drips from the endless rain, and she pulls me aside.

"You don't need to contact the fundamentals," she says quietly. "I know the only way to wake Water."

"What? How?" I had assumed it was a job for Air and Fire, so I hadn't inquired about the process. I stare at Minnie, whose eyes are filled with a mixture of pain and acceptance that I don't understand. She touches my cheek with a soft hand.

"I spoke to Shannon on Tuesday night, after we found out you could become the earth fundamental. She told me who my father is. He's the water fundamental, in the same way your father was the earth fundamental. Water is now in half-dormancy so that I can live."

183

This is an unexpected angle. My eyes rake across Minnie's face, searching for answers.

"Why would he do that, after seeing mine be in half-dormancy for so long?"

Minnie shrugs.

"Curiosity, I think. The elementals really like visiting our world, and I guess the fundamentals are no different. They have the power to come across, too, so the temptation must always be there." She shakes her head quickly as if to clear it. "Anyway, I'm his daughter, and to bring him back to full power, I need to give up my elemental side to make sure the balance is maintained."

"All right," I say, still not understanding why Minnie looks so sad. "We pass him your elemental side. You've been having trouble with personality shifts lately. Perhaps this is an opportunity."

She shakes her head sadly before I can finish my words.

"It's not that simple. My two sides are intertwined, Shannon was telling me about it. I can't survive if they are disconnected, just like you can't be a fully elemental fundamental. My two sides are inseparable in this body."

"What are you saying?" I whisper, but the squeezing of my heart is leading me down the path of truth. I don't want to follow it there.

"I have to die," she says. Despite the pelting rain, a tear visibly spills from her eye and trails down her cheek.

I step back involuntarily. I'm reeling from those four simple words, and my mind grinds to a halt.

I can't lose Minnie. Centuries of feeling alone, even when I haven't been, well up inside. Reuniting with Minnie and realizing that she is all my loves from my past filled me with the sharpest painful joy that I have ever experienced.

But it was only a few short months ago. We have had

scarcely a moment together compared to the vastness of my life.

"No," I say hoarsely. I'm vaguely aware of the others chattering nearby, but my focus is on Minnie. "No. There has to be another way."

"I promise, there isn't."

"I can't lose you." My fists clench and unclench in my desire to do something, anything, to change those four words Minnie said. "We just found each other. We only got married last week. I can't give you up, not so soon."

Minnie steps forward and takes my hands in her own. She gazes at me with those big blue eyes. My horror at her words must have strengthened her own resolve, for the sorrow that tormented her face moments ago has shifted to acceptance.

"We can be together again," she says softly. "You have the grail now so you can wake me up when I appear. You know I'll always find you."

"No." My head shakes my rejection, and I can't stop it. "No."

"You have to become the earth fundamental," she says, a stern note in her voice. "This will be a short separation for a good cause. You need to do this, for the world and for yourself. I will come back. I always do." She looks down at my fingers and strokes them with her own, then she looks up at me again. "I don't think we would work in this lifetime, anyway. Our elemental sides are not compatible. You saw the way they don't even want to touch anymore, and it's only growing worse with your stretching." She nods at our strands, which press against our own bodies to avoid each other's. "What will it be like when you're the fundamental? Let me go, and we'll be together again in the future, but properly this time."

"I don't understand. Why are you pushing this? You're going to die. Why are you so accepting?"

185

"It's easier to die when I know I'll be reborn." Minnie gives me a half-smile and lays her hand on my cheek. "And when I know you'll be there, waiting for me."

"But Xenia came out of dormancy without me needing to die," I say desperately. "Can't Water do the same?"

"Water knows that the ramifications of coming out of half-dormancy are disastrous. Because of Xenia's escape and the imbalance it caused, the elemental plane is in chaos, and our world isn't far behind. Another fundamental in full power would be catastrophic."

"Incoming," Wayne shouts. "Xenia's here."

I glance toward the temple. Xenia strides from the dark stone archway into the dimming light, her ceremonial headdress gone and her skirt and tunic unadorned with precious gems. She has come to fight, and she is ready.

I have never been less ready. I don't know what to do. The only way to stop her—according to Minnie, the other fundamentals, and the feeling in my gut—is to let Minnie die to bring Water out of dormancy. Only with the three fundamentals will Xenia be defeated and her power transferred to me.

But I don't want that power, not if it means giving up Minnie.

The ground shakes with the first tremors. Xenia is smiling, her eyes wild. She doesn't think there is a chance she'll be defeated, not by our ragtag group. She's right. We need the fundamentals.

And I need the purpose that being the fundamental would give me. My whole outlook changed when I heard that news. It felt so right that I wondered how I had managed to fumble along for so many centuries without knowing the joy of direction. Could I go back to that state if Minnie were at my side?

Xenia yanks at a clump of lauvan, and two pillars of earth fly into the air, narrowly missing Jen and buckling Alejandro's leg. Xenia laughs and pulls again. We all jump out of the way when the ground rolls toward us.

"Let's run away together," I yell to Minnie desperately. My hand squeezes hers so tightly that I'm afraid I'll break something. "Forget this mess. We can deal with the chaos as it comes."

"The world can't deal with it," Minnie shouts back. "You need to embrace this. Become the earth fundamental, this is what you were born to be. Then you can bring balance back and save so many. It's up to you, and you alone." We dive to the side to avoid another dirt wave and roll together. When we stop, she lies on top of me in a sorry reflection of better times. She kisses me once, hard, then gazes into my eyes. "We will be together again."

My friends shout around us and the earth shakes. I stare at Minnie. She's right. I do need this. I could give it all up and run away with Minnie, but that's not the kind of man I want to be. Alejandro's actions of late, and of all his past lives, float to the surface of my mind. Perhaps it's time for the teacher to become the student. I want to learn from him, become a better man than I am. Doing the right thing here, embracing my purpose, will be the first step.

I imagine what the centuries of terrible loneliness and aimlessness might have been like if I had had a reason for being, besides waiting for Arthur to return. Would my days have been spent looking forward with hope instead of backward with longing?

Something must change in my eyes because Minnie pats my chest.

"Good man," she says. "We need to get to where the earth cable meets the water. Come on."

187

CHAPTER XXI

She climbs off me and I roll to my feet. A pillar of earth flies at my face, and I narrowly avoid having my teeth knocked out by ducking and yanking lauvan as hard as I can. Mud sprays in all directions, but the pillar crumbles.

"Come on," Minnie shouts and grabs my hand. We run toward the ocean, dozens of paces away, but a wall of mud slices the air before us. We skid to a halt, and I whip my head around.

Xenia strides toward me, her face twisted with manic glee and her hands lifted as if in supplication. Her chestnut brown strands swirl around her in a cloud so wild that I expect to see lightning bolts fly out of it.

"Going somewhere?" she calls out in a mockery of March's low voice. "I did hope you would put up a fight. Controlling the humans is too easy. I like a challenge. Not that you'll provide much of one, but beggars can't be choosers."

I don't bother talking. Xenia isn't worth my breath, and I have other things to consider, like how I will take her by surprise. My mind races as I gather air lauvan around me. It might not be my element of choice, but keeping Xenia on her toes means working outside my comfort zone and hers. Despite her quest to learn all she can about life as a half-elemental, I have been practicing for centuries.

When I have a substantial clump of the insubstantial air strands in my fists, I gather my intention to blast whatever earth attack Xenia's narrowed eyes are currently concocting. My heart squeezes when Minnie brushes my back, and a wave of despair nearly undoes me. Will that be the last time she touches me, the last time I hear her quiet breath in my ear?

"Go," she whispers. "I'll follow with water."

I rip my thoughts away from my grief and channel my intentions into the lauvan. The threads sail away from me as Xenia thrusts her hands forward and sends an explosion of gravel toward us like a shotgun blast. The air meets it halfway and the gravel bursts upward and back to Xenia, who deflects it with an air barrier of her own. Minnie's jet of water bounces harmlessly off.

Xenia raises her arms then screams with pain and outrage. Unseen by her, Anna crawled from behind and scratched her leg with a shard of sharp rock. Blood wells from the wound, and I marvel at Anna's courage. Now, strands from the amulet she planted on Xenia will be fully activated, and March can push harder from her side. Every little tactic that weakens Xenia is a triumph. If there were any doubt about Anna's loyalty, she proved herself today.

March's burgundy lauvan that swirl around Xenia's body boil and twist, but Xenia ignores them. She whirls around and pulls earth strands up with a vindictive grimace. The earth below Anna punches upward, and Anna's body flings in a wide arc toward the others.

"Run." Minnie pulls my arm. There is no time to see if Anna is all right. "We need to get to the water."

I gather air lauvan as we go, and it's a good thing I do. Before we take two steps, a crunching sound makes me fling the air threads backward. Stones the size of my head ricochet off the hastily erected barrier, and my blood runs cold at our close call. What would I do if Minnie were killed by an errant rock?

Then I remember that she must die today, and my feet stumble as my entire body seizes at the ghastly thought.

Is there any other way to defeat Xenia without Minnie dying? I wrack my brains desperately, but no options present themselves. Without passing Minnie's elemental lauvan to

189

Water, the fundamentals won't be strong enough to take Xenia back to their plane of existence. With her elemental strands ripped from her body, Minnie will die.

A few more steps down the embankment, then Minnie and I are blasted off our feet. A burst of air like the shockwave of a bomb flings us away from the ocean. I fling my hands out to break my fall, and my palms grind against rock with painful scrapes. Minnie falls next to me, although she looks back immediately afterward. My ears ring from the pressure, and I turn.

The air minions are back on their feet, no doubt healed by Xenia.

"We've got the minions," Alejandro yells at me. "Focus on Xenia!"

"Yes, focus on me," Xenia sneers. "I'm sure you can handle it."

The rock we kneel on cracks in the middle. I shout and leap to Minnie before the crevasse can separate us. Minnie's eyes are wide, and her face is splattered with mud, but she twists a ball of blue lauvan in her hands with steady motions.

"Distract her," she says quietly. I don't hesitate but turn and stand.

"You think a little hole in the ground is going to cut it?' I yell. "I've seen the true power of a fundamental. You're only toying with us."

Xenia smiles.

"Of course. Why would I bother raising my arm when a finger will do? If I wished, the earth could swallow you in an instant. But what fun would that be?"

I yank the earth lauvan at my feet and hurl rocks her way. Xenia dodges them gracefully, laughing while she does it. Minnie releases her water trick, and hundreds of needle-sharp icicles lance toward Xenia.

Xenia's eyes widen. With a twist of her fingers, she constructs a barrier bubble around herself. The icicles embed in the barrier then melt instantly.

Minnie pulls my arm, and we stumble toward the ocean once more. The shore is only a dozen paces away, but it feels like an insurmountable distance.

"I need a water cable to transfer my lauvan to my father," Minnie says to me in the brief second we have before Xenia gathers herself.

"We're almost there," I pant, but fire licks around my feet, and we leap backward in shock.

"Being a fundamental," Xenia says from behind us. "And a half-elemental, and a worshiped being, translates into being able to do whatever I want. Bow before me, underling. You don't have a chance."

I turn, enraged at constantly being thwarted by my enemy. I'm racing to a goal that I don't even want—the death of my beloved wife—and Xenia won't get out of my way.

"I bow to no one," I hiss and gather strands around me. I'm indiscriminate, and the ball of lauvan that I collect has strands of water, earth, air, and even a little fire from the blaze that Xenia created between me and the shore. I don't know what it will do, but I'm past caring.

I throw the ball at Xenia as her hands are full of whatever punishment she plans to mete out. The ball hits her on the arm and explodes.

Xenia screams in rage and pain. Her arm flings backward as shards of rock, jets of water, blasts of air, and sparks of flame burst from the ball and dig into her soft flesh. A flicker of satisfaction peeks through the fog of my despair. Xenia can be hurt. I will use that knowledge.

I run sideways with Minnie to get around the wall of fire, but Xenia's shriek echoes behind us.

191

"You will pay for that!"

The ground below us breaks into a disk of rock that shoots skyward. Minnie and I hold on with whitened, bleeding knuckles. We fly up and shoot toward the temple, whose open courtyard is visible from this terrifying angle. Screams filter through the air, and with an effort I turn my head. Similar disks of stone soar behind us with other figures splayed on their tops.

There's no time to look further. Minnie screams as we descend to the courtyard. Just before we crash onto stone pavers, I leap up and twist an air barrier below us. The impact is jarring, but our bones are spared. The same can't be said for the rock, which cracks into three sharp pieces.

Other disks come flying from the opening, and I use our lauvan connections to pull my friends in my direction, away from the crashing rock.

"Air barrier," I shout to Minnie, and she swiftly constructs a rudimentary one before Wayne and Anna barrel into us, closely followed by the rest.

"Is everyone all right?" I ask. Beside wide eyes and streaks of blood, no one appears to be seriously wounded.

"Now, what?" Jen says in a shaky voice.

"Minnie and I need to get to the ocean," I say. "It's the only way to summon the water fundamental."

I have to choke out the last word. Deathbed memories flicker through my mind like a badly edited movie. All the women Minnie used to be die before my eyes, and I am powerless to stop them. Each memory hits me like a punch to the stomach, and I can scarcely breathe.

Minnie grips my arm tightly. Perhaps she sees the panic in my eyes. She was always perceptive.

In the stillness of the temple, without enemies to fight, the others gaze around in fright and awe.

"This place is incredible," Wayne murmurs. "Too bad it's

192

for worshiping a psychopath."

Stone walls soar above us in a space large enough for a crowd but small enough that it feels like we're at the end of a tube with the roof opening to the distant sky. The darkness of approaching nightfall makes it hard to see details in the gloom. Pillars are embedded at each corner of the square space, and inset alcoves flank dark passageways in each wall. Lines and detailed carvings around each alcove are extraordinarily intricate. Each alcove ensconces a statue of Xenia, and I shake my head in amazement.

The stone, however, is not the most incredible sight. Every surface is covered with a shifting layer of multicolored lauvan. The temple itself must be infused with power from Xenia's devotees. If this is the excess, I shudder to think of how much she has stored on her person.

Jen opens her mouth to speak, but shouting makes her pause.

"They're coming," says Alejandro. He positions himself near the open archway from where the sound drifts in. "Prepare yourselves. Minnie and Merry can take on Xenia, like before, and the rest of us work on the followers and air minions. Got it?"

The others nod with pale, determined faces. I hate putting them through this, but I can't imagine anyone else I would rather have at my side.

Well, a few hundred sturdy warriors with battle axes wouldn't hurt, but I am content with my friends.

"Minnie." I turn to her. Her beautiful face looks at mine in question, and the thought of never seeing her face again, of having to wait twenty or thirty years—or perhaps longer—to meet her again, closes my throat in its intensity. That's assuming I even find her at all. I shudder but manage to push words out of my tight chest. "Whatever you do, run to the ocean, all right? We need to summon Water. I'll be right

193

behind you."

Minnie nods. Her eyes search mine, and her fingers stroke my cheek with a feather touch.

"I don't want to die by myself," she whispers so only I can hear. Pounding footsteps on stone flagstones alert us to the arrival of Xenia's people. I clutch the back of her head and press my lips tightly to her forehead, overcome.

"I'll be there," I say. "Until the very end."

Xenia's followers, the devotees that worshiped her without compulsion, run screaming into the courtyard. Xenia must have healed them for cannon fodder. Their eyes are wild, and they brandish picks and shovels. Their choice of weapons would make me laugh if they didn't swing them with such determined force. The air minions follow behind. Their eyes scan the area with a calculated gleam, contrasting sharply with the devotees' manic glints.

Alejandro yells wordlessly and charges toward the devotees. Wayne and the others follow. The tranquilizer guns must be out of darts because Cecil now brandishes a pickax and Wayne a sledgehammer, likely found around the work yard. Jen has picked up a hammer from somewhere, and Anna still swings her baseball bat with precision.

Xenia isn't yet in sight, so Minnie and I run around the melee to target the air minions. The woman is preparing to blast my friends with wind, but a jet of water to her face knocks her over, spluttering. The male minion retaliates by ramming us off our feet with a gust of air, but from my grounded position, the earth lauvan are ready and waiting. With a yank, the stone pavers under his feet crumble. He drops to the floor, yelling with pain and clutching his ankle.

"Welcome to the human body," I shout at him. "Pain's a bitch."

Minnie touches my shoulder.

194

"Let's go," she says. "The others can handle the humans."

"Go where?" a voice from the archway says smoothly.

I turn with trepidation. Xenia stalks toward us, anger and focus in her gaze.

"Go," I say to Minnie urgently. "Get to the water. I'll find my way there soon."

Minnie wavers, but at a push from me she darts toward another pillared archway on the side. Xenia laughs.

"So chivalrous," she says. "It doesn't matter what your little half-elemental concubine does. It's you I want to conquer. At first, it was amusing to watch you blunder about, and this pitched battle was rather fun, but I'm getting bored. This human body of mine is telling me that it's past time for a late dinner." Xenia gestures to the pillars that are surrounded by lauvan of every color. "What do you think of my decorating? This temple is a repository of power. All I need to do is touch it."

Xenia places her hand on the pillar and closes her eyes. The strands flow from their position over rock and onto her body. Faster and faster they gather around her, until her form is barely visible through the swirling maelstrom of threads that pulse with their own rhythm like a giant multicolored heart. With one, final writhe in unison, they tint a uniform chestnut brown. Xenia's face appears in the cloud, and she opens her eyes and smiles.

"And I bring it into myself. Ingenious, no? It is astonishing what one can learn when one is stuck in dormancy with only stories to amuse oneself."

I need to distract Xenia long enough to make my escape. Minnie waits for me on the shores of the sea and reaching her is the only way to put an end to Xenia. How can I divert her attention?

My lessons with Tremor and Quake filter into my mind, and

an idea percolates.

"Ingenious, indeed," I say. With a pull of strands, the rock beneath me cracks open. Below, I can sense dirt underneath cracked foundation. I pull it toward me swiftly and lay a pile of soil on the pavers. Xenia watches me with curiosity. "But I wonder if you have heard this tale?"

With a few quick twists and a strand of my own woven into the pattern, a man-sized golem pushes to its feet before me. My energy plummets, but I maintain the connection. Xenia's eyes widen with surprise, and I don't waste my opportunity. The golem charges and I run sideways toward the arch that Minnie disappeared through.

A blast of air pulses past me, and clods of dirt fly. Energy returns to me, and my heart sinks when I realize that my golem must be destroyed. I hoped that it would distract her for longer.

I race through winding passageways made entirely of stone blocks. I feel like a tunneling creature, but the sensation isn't unpleasant. I understand why Xenia constructed her temple the way she did.

Where is the exit? I need to get to Minnie.

"What a marvelous idea," Xenia shouts behind me.

I curse and run faster. Of course, she knows the way through her own temple better than I do. I reach a dead end and press my hands against the wall in hopeless panic. The few threads of rainbow lauvan that flutter above the stone weave into my hand.

Can I take some of the strands to increase my own power? I have only seconds to spare, but I pull the strands toward me with all the intention I can muster. The closest ones race to my hands and wind themselves around my own lauvan. A ticklish moment later, they are all chocolate brown.

I have no more time to experiment. I turn back to the previous crossroads with panic lodged in my throat. Xenia's voice is closer behind me as I run along the next tunnel.

"I have heard the tale of how our predecessors animated their elements," she calls out. "Thanks for the idea. I might use it."

Finally, the tunnel lightens. I burst through the entryway with relief.

Cracking, grating sounds leak from the stone behind me. With a sinking heart, I turn to look.

The walls of the temple nearest me are breaking apart, splintering and cracking into moving forms that rise three times higher than my head. My mouth drops.

Xenia made stone golems, and they are coming for me.

CHAPTER XXII

Faint screaming from the water's edge alerts me to Minnie's presence, but the groans of crushing stone almost obliterates the sound.

I was hoping that Xenia would take my golem bait—a golem will drain her of energy, and every advantage of power I can gain over her is one step closer to my goals—but I don't know what to do against massive stone golems. My mind blanks of any counterattacks. I need to get to Minnie. This is out of my hands now—we need the fundamentals to take Xenia away. I am only one man, abilities or not.

I turn to run, but the two golems are swifter than they appear. A massive stone appendage, too blunt to be called a fist, sweeps toward me. I barely have time to dive to the side before it passes over me and brushes the back of my coat. I scramble to my feet, but the slippery ground costs me precious seconds. With the sound of whistling movement, another appendage soars my way.

Contact is brutal. The stone fist flings me across the paved front terrace. An instant of numbness disappears in midair when piercing pain overwhelms me. My arm and chest are on fire. When I land on the stone pavers a second later, the impact jars my injuries. I scream at the agony as it rips through my body.

My eyes are screwed shut to ward off the pain, but I can't afford that. Thunderous footsteps pound the stone below my body, and I push up from the ground. Another scream rips out of my hoarse throat and my vision tunnels at the motion of my broken arm and fractured ribs.

I can still breathe, barely, and my legs still work, so I stumble forward. The footsteps are right behind me now, so when I hear the whoosh of a giant arm once more, I dart sideways. The arm flings past me without contact. As I suspected, the golem is strong but not nimble. I can work with that.

I run forward, massaging the knots on my useless arm with my fingers. If I can at least numb the pain, I can think. If I can think, I will have a chance to escape this new threat.

I leap sideways, away from the next fist. I'm too slow, but a gust of air catches me off guard and flings me to the side. The golem's fist crashes into the stone pavers directly where I stood a moment before, and bits of rock fly past my face.

Silver threads dart away, and I shake my head to clear it. Are the elementals helping me? Air and Fire said they would do what they could to tip the scales. Is this what they meant?

I'll take whatever help I can get. The pain in my arm is slightly less from my massaging, although the appendage is still unusable. I narrowly avoid another golem fist, and it nudges my back with the gentleness of a stampeding horse. I stumble forward and finally regain my feet with the nudge of a cluster of silver threads.

Minnie is still so far away, and I don't know how to get to her in time. Making the golem was a mistake. Everything I try, Xenia can do a hundred times more effectively, and her power seems scarcely diminished by the effort. She has the means to finish me for good.

But I can't let that happen. If I don't survive, Minnie will be reborn, but I won't be waiting for her. That thought pains me more than my cracked ribs. I can't leave her alone. I know too well that sorrow. Not that she will know, but what if she feels an unidentifiable loss her entire life? She has never left me. It's my duty to stick around for her.

Another fist punches through the air at me. I turn around and leap at the golem's leg. My fingers desperately wrench a strand from my body and try to weave it into the golem to take control of the rock monster, but Xenia shouts in anger.

"Are you trying to steal my animation?"

Lauvan surrounding the golem pulses with power, and I am blasted off the creature. Only a cushion of air threads from helper elementals prevents my head from cracking against pavers. Xenia poured more of herself into the golems, and there is no way I can take them over now.

This isn't working. I need to get to Minnie and end this.

Power bubbles in me from the extra lauvan I siphoned off the temple. Can I use it to increase my abilities? I race away, collecting air and water strands as I go. When my functioning hand has gathered enough of each, I fling them back at Xenia. With the extra power I infuse into them, they balloon into a whirling maelstrom of torrential, biting rain. With another yank to nearby earth lauvan, I create a crack in the stone that a running Xenia falls into.

I don't wait to see the aftermath.

Minnie is only a dozen paces away now, standing thigh-deep in the steely gray ocean water. Every time a wave crashes through her, she shudders from the cold. She stands next to the earth cable that plunges into the sea. The cable's light flickers over her in the deepening gloom of night.

I jump into frothing surf from a shallow retaining wall onto a base of pebbly sand and push through the dense water toward her. Closer, her shuddering is clearly visible, but it's not only from the frigid cold that bites into our skin with venom. Her eyes are frightened, and her lips are tight.

"You're hurt," she says with a glance at my arm. I shake my head.

"It doesn't matter. There's no time to heal it."

"I'm scared," she whispers and hugs herself.

Tears spring into my eyes and I wrap her in my one good

arm, heedless of the pain my cracked ribs shoot through my torso. The agony in my heart is far worse. I thought having to watch her die—again—would be the worst thing I'd see today, but watching her shiver with fear at the prospect is unbearable.

"I thought I could do it," she says, gesturing to the ocean. "Call Water to finish this. But I can't. I told myself that I was only waiting for you to be with me, but that's a lie. I can't do it."

"There has to be another way," I mutter. "Can we not join elemental forces like we did a few weeks ago? That cable knocked her senseless."

"We had Todd with us then. We're missing his air and fire to our earth and water. It wouldn't work."

"Then let's run away together," I say desperately. I can't see her like this, not for anything. "Someone else can be the fundamental. They'll figure it out. How much chaos would the world be in, really?" I don't believe my words, but I need to comfort Minnie somehow.

Strangely, my words light a spark in her eyes. She stands straight and drops her hands to her sides.

"No," she says clearly. "We need to do this."

"Do we?" I know the answer, but I need Minnie to choose it. I don't care how much the world will suffer. I will not force this on anyone who is less than willing. The world needs me to take on the role of fundamental and defeat Xenia—I need to—but none of that matters unless Minnie agrees. It must be her choice.

She nods, and my heart squeezes as if the stone golem has mashed it flat.

"Let's do this."

She kisses me in the pounding spray, shouts of our friends and enemies echoing in the distance, and I memorize the shape of her lips, the feel of her body against mine, the taste of her mouth. When a grating roar echoes behind me, I part from Minnie for the last time.

"I had you pegged for the clingy type," she says softly, a smile on her face despite the tears that mingle with rain on her cheeks. "I guess I had that wrong."

I can't make a sound, no matter how hard I try. Minnie reaches into the waves and narrows her eyes in concentration. I look at the shore, and the two golems are striding our way with thunderous steps, Xenia between them. Her brown strands crackle with energy in a vicious cloud around her body. When I turn back, Minnie has a water cable in her arms.

"I'm ready," she says clearly. "I love you, Merry Lytton."

"I love you too," I croak out. "Forever and always."

Minnie smiles.

"What are you doing?" Xenia says. For the first time, she sounds genuinely concerned. I turn to her hateful face with the golems towering over her.

"Getting rid of you once and for all," I shout. "Not even you stand a chance against the combined might of Water, Fire, and Air. Then I will be fundamental, and you will be dormant forever."

Xenia's eyes widen, and she glances at Minnie before her eyes flicker to me again.

"I see," she says in a different voice. "You are more cunning than I thought. More heartless, too. I thought the bonds of human love were stronger than this, but you are only half-human, after all. As for the cunning, no doubt the other fundamentals are behind this. I don't blame you for siding with them, Merry. For one so small as you, it can be hard to resist those with so much power."

"I'm done talking," I say. "Water needs to be reawakened, and you need to be sent to dormancy."

"Wait!" Xenia pushes her hand through the mess of brown

202

lauvan in a stopping gesture. "The fundamentals are worried about balance. I understand. Water must emerge, and Earth must take its place in the elemental plane once more. But there is no need for you to become fundamental. I will willingly go and perform my duty as earth fundamental. Your woman will still die, of course." Xenia glances at Minnie behind me. "But I have the power to bring her back immediately. In a different body, of course, but an adult one. If you relinquish your claim to my fundamental role, I will bring her back to you within the week."

Xenia must understand the predicament she is in and the power I wield. But her words give me pause. Could Minnie come back right away? Do I trust Xenia to return to her state as earth fundamental in the elemental plane? Can I allow my new purpose to drift away from me so easily? These questions swirl in my mind as I stare into Xenia's eyes. She searches mine for answers.

"Don't trust her," Minnie whispers. "This is the only way."

I tuck my numb left arm under Minnie's, and she grips it fiercely. I reach out my right.

"We humans shake on deals," I say loudly. "Come, show me you're genuine."

Xenia's face breaks into a smile. She leaves her hulking golems on the shore and wades into the crashing waves. Her brilliant purple skirt soaks to her knees immediately.

She reaches me, hesitates, then grasps my hand with a firm grip. Her strands cover my arm. I squeeze tightly and yell.

"Now, March! Fight!"

I swing Xenia around until we are both in the earth cable. Through some instinct, Minnie sweeps the water cable close until all three of us and the two cables intersect. There is a massive pulse of power, and my newly stretched self welcomes it.

The ocean froths with mad wavelets in a whirlpool around the three of us, and a howling windstorm presses in. Crackling fireballs, reminiscent of ball lightning, appear out of nowhere and circle our group with terrifying intensity. The smell of burning sulfur fills my nose.

The fundamentals might not be able to enter our world without disrupting the balance, but they have sent their emissaries to help as much as they can. The three of us are trapped in their net, and there is only one way out.

With all my intent, I enter the lauvan world and entwine my strands with Xenia's copious elemental ones to pull her toward Minnie.

There is a push from the body—March is there, fighting hard, strengthened by Anna's spell—and a pull from Minnie. Minnie, clever woman that she is, has grasped my plan and helps with all her might. While Xenia is still in March's body, she has access to the extra power from her worshipers. With her removed from that source, we might have a chance.

It wouldn't work if Xenia weren't weakened. Anna's amulet enables March to fight her from the inside, and Xenia's strands fuel the two massive golems on the shore. She used much of her power to animate them and left her core self weak. Despite her diminished state, she fights with all her might.

A great rushing flows around us, and we are surrounded by silver and orange strands. Little by little, we force Xenia's strands out of March's body and into Minnie's. If Minnie must die, then I sure as hell won't let Xenia survive. It makes me sick to see Xenia's chestnut brown strands intermingling with Minnie's midnight blue ones. When the last strand leaves March's body, I enter my body again.

The golems are raging above me, their featureless heads terrifying without expressions. One has its fist raised to smash down on us.

"Together, Minnie!" I yell. With all my intent, I grab her shoulders and force my will on the golems through her. Because Xenia is now a part of Minnie, and her strands power the golems, Minnie and I can now control them.

A handspan away from hitting us, the golem's fist stops. Slowly, it retreats, stomps to the shore, and stands motionless with its companion. They stare blankly out to sea.

Chestnut brown strands fly from the golems toward Minnie. Xenia is collecting all her lauvan to make a final push. I look into Minnie's eyes, and I can see the exact moment that Xenia wages war on Minnie for control of the body.

Minnie still clutches the water cable, but her arms slacken around it. She's losing the battle for supremacy. I can't let Minnie's sacrifice be in vain. Xenia cannot win, and she especially cannot control my beautiful wife's body. The thought turns my stomach, and I reach into Minnie's center.

Xenia's brown strands are skittish, but I grip them with firm fingers and pull. Minnie's eyes roll, then they snap to my face. She nods then closes her eyes. A sob breaks from me, and for the millionth time I rack my brain for another option.

A stream of midnight blue flows out through the water cable. Xenia's chestnut brown strands cover Minnie's body despite my hold on them. Minnie's elemental strands are leaving, and Xenia is taking over. I yank at Xenia's strands desperately, but she has inhuman strength. I can't hold her back from taking over Minnie's body for much longer, but I must or else Minnie's sacrifice will be for nothing.

There's a roar in the distance. Are Xenia's golems waking up again? Seaward motion catches my eye, and I stare at a wall of water barreling down at us. Minnie's departing strands awakened Water. The wave is so close, and there is no time to move. I hold my breath, clutch Minnie's body to my chest with my good arm, and close my eyes as the wave crashes down.

CHAPTER XXIII

Bitingly cold water hits my face and forces me onto my back. Everything spins, and I don't know what is up or down. The only certainty is Minnie's warm body in my arms, and I squeeze her tightly to my chest as the wave rolls us uncontrollably. My injured arm scrapes against the seafloor, but the pain only makes me grip Minnie more securely.

My lungs burn, but my heart burns hotter and with greater pain. I almost welcome the cold chaos to numb the agony of truth.

Finally, the water stops tossing us around, and my head bursts above the waves. I gasp a blissful gulp of air then find my feet. It's not deep—despite the tossing and flailing, we didn't travel far—and I carefully raise Minnie's head until it is above the water.

Splashing alerts me to another's presence, but I have eyes only for Minnie. Xenia's chestnut brown strands are gone, removed from the physical world by the water fundamental. Minnie's slender elemental lauvan are gone, too, and only a few of her thicker human ones remain. As I watch, threads of midnight blue float into the air and fade, one by one, until only a few limp strands cling to her body.

Minnie is gone, and I can't bring her back.

Someone grips my shoulder and shakes it gently. There are words, but I can't comprehend the meaning. All I see is Minnie's still, pale face, startlingly free of blue threads. I'm too numb for tears, too deep in this fog to hear the others.

The hand on my shoulder turns into a supportive arm that leads me shoreward. Through the numbness, I realize it is Cecil. Bodies lie on the shore, and I recognize the closest one as March. She might have survived had she been possessed by a weaker elemental than Xenia. March pushed hard at the end, and it was thanks to her that we were able to defeat the fundamental. Regret sweeps through my body at March's unneeded death. She and I never saw eye to eye, but I wouldn't have wished that end on anyone.

We climb onto the bank and Alejandro runs toward us, closely followed by Jen. They babble words, words, so many words, but I can't hear any of them. My injured arm isn't strong enough to haul Minnie's body out of the water, but I can't let her go. Alejandro supports her body and gently pushes my arm away. He carries her to the retaining wall and lays her carefully down on the ground beyond.

I'm still in the water, staring after Minnie. Jen appears in my vision, and it takes a huge amount of willpower to force myself to look at her tear-streaked face, but her words don't penetrate.

My gaze travels around the scene of devastation. The temple is in ruins, great chunks ripped out of it where the golems burst forth. The wide expanse of carefully laid pavers in beautiful patterns are ripped up into mounds of dirt and debris. Bodies lie at awkward angles, and not all of them have living lauvan attached. The golems are only piles of rubble on the shore now that Xenia's power has left them.

My eyes drift to my right where the earth cable dips into the sea. Earth. Lauvan. Elementals.

My mind suddenly revs up. The reason Minnie died, the reason Xenia was taken away, it was all to ensure that I became the next fundamental. I know through instinct that I need to connect to complete my task. It's the last thing I feel like doing, but Minnie's lifeless face draws my eye once more. Why is she dead, if not for this? She fulfilled her duty, and it cost her life. I must do my part.

I push Jen out of the way and stumble to the cable. Before I can think too hard or prepare myself, my good hand plunges into the flowing mass of brown.

Not this time the blissful pain of a cable for me. Instead, I am blasted by the full power of earth. Screaming pierces my ears through the wall of sound and it takes a moment to realize that it's me. Sensations bombard me from every earth phenomena that exists. The explosive power of an earthquake, the grating roar of a landslide, the plinking drop of a tiny pebble, the rasping scrape of sand on a beach, the suffocating flow of mud, even the deepest grinding slide of tectonic plates, all flow into me without filter. All the ages of the Earth pass through me, from the first meteors that bombarded the molten planet, to fiery volcanoes that covered the surface, to floating continents, rising and falling mountains, and scraping glaciers.

I am overwhelmed with no clue what is happening or when it will end. It feels like forever and yet no time at all.

Eventually, the sensations pull back and finish. I'm left gasping with my arm extended into the now-innocuous cable that glimmers innocently at me. Every part of me feels full to bursting, excruciating compared to the ache of stretching, and I'm suddenly grateful for the sessions with Tremor and Quake. Without the stretching I would be dead, I have no doubt. I hope I loosen over time because this power within me is distressingly tight.

I look back, and my friends watch me with fearful eyes. My gaze travels to Minnie's supine form, and I am overwhelmed once more, but this time by grief instead of earthen sensations. I didn't think there would be room for any more feeling, yet there the grief is, making space for itself in the mess of my heart.

I know what happened had to happen, but my failure to protect my love is a sword in my gut that twists with every passing second. Protecting Minnie was my duty as her husband, my pleasure as her lover, and my calling as her friend. She might have chosen her path with clear eyes and conviction, but it doesn't make the pain any easier to bear nor my failure any less shameful.

Alejandro is the first one to approach me. His face is filled with concern, but the fear has faded. He was always the bravest of us in the ways that matter.

"Is it over?" he asks in a tentative voice.

I nod, unsure if my tongue even works after my ordeal. I glance at Minnie again.

"Almost," I rasp out.

I take slow, uncertain steps toward the group. Everything is tight and painful, and it feels like I'm learning how to walk again. My body doesn't know what to do with this power and will have to learn. It's not my pressing concern right now.

The others part for me to reach Minnie's side. I bend on stiff knees and look at my beautiful wife for the last time. She looks peaceful, even serene, though her lack of lauvan makes her appear unbalanced and oddly naked to my eyes. I touch her soft cheek, and the motion nearly undoes me.

"See you soon," I whisper, then I twist the last remaining strands at her center.

Her body dissolves into a fine, powdery dust that collects in a pile where her center used to be. Before it can get too wet from the pelting rain, I grab a nearby air thread.

"Air," I say in a loud, hoarse voice. "I need you."

An overwhelming presence in the lauvan tells me that the air fundamental is here.

"Take her ashes to this lake in the mountains," I say and send Air directions through my intentions. "Scatter them over the surface."

A gentle breeze, so different from the howling winds during our battle with the air minions, passes over the ashes. I let go of the air thread and watch Minnie's remains flutter through the sky in a stream of pale dust that twists and twirls northward until it is lost to the darkness.

When it is finally gone, my shoulders slump.

"Come on, Merry," Wayne's gruff voice says. His hand grips my good arm firmly and hauls me up. "Let's get away from here."

I don't resist as he leads me up the steep gravel driveway, down the road, and to the van. Chloe's face appears in the window, frightened and relieved at once. She scans our group then flings the back door open.

"Where's Minnie?" she asks in a high-pitched voice. Anna shushes her and bends to whisper in her ear.

I don't look at Chloe as Wayne settles me in the passenger's seat. I know she will have pity, horror, maybe tears there, and I don't want to see it. All I want to do is go home and sleep. The thought of my home without Minnie in it threatens to slice my heart in two, but I push the emotion away. There is no room in my body for sharp grief. I need to preserve the numbness as long as I can.

Jen climbs into the driver's seat and starts the van. As we pull away from the curb, sirens wail. Through the fog in my mind, I wonder what Officer Lee will make of this. She never called in the special unit for cults that she threatened to. I expect I'll hear from her in the future.

Jen drops off the others at Alejandro and Liam's house. I think about offering to heal their injuries, but by the time I muster up the energy to speak, Jen has already pulled into traffic. I lean back against the headrest and work out the knots in my own broken arm while she drives. If anyone were in mortal danger, they would have said something.

"I'm going to stay at your place tonight," Jen announces. She glances at me for a reaction, so I nod to show her I heard. She can do what she likes. I can't find it in myself to take an interest in her whereabouts, although there is a sliver of gratitude that she cares enough to stay. I will try to hold onto that.

CHAPTER XXIV

Dreaming

I glance sideways at my companion, a large, blustering mountain of a man with a round stomach and a rich laugh to match. His graying hair is wild around the temples and flaps in the wind as we stride across the university courtyard.

"Thank you for the kind invite to sup with you tonight, Master Edmundas," I say. A passing student bows his head at Edmundas in deference and he nods back with a genial smile. "I know few people in the city, since I am so new here."

"I thought as much. My wife orders a good repast, never fear." He pats his stomach and chuckles. "Too good. I've invited a few other professors tonight, Masters Donatas and Kristupas, so you might know them better and the conversation be more stimulating."

"How thoughtful." It has only been a week since I arrived at the newly established Vilnian Academy, and I'm already chafing at my lack of companionship. Tonight will serve as a casual introduction to faculty at the university. I'm not the only new professor here, but connecting is not a simple matter.

"Where did they steal you from, again? I'm certain you told me, but it has already slipped my mind."

"I taught the trivium at Heidelberg, in Germany."

"Ah, grammar, logic, and rhetoric. The fundamentals of any fine education. I give lectures on philosophy, myself. What drew you to Vilnian?"

"I could hardly refuse the salary they offered, especially as I have no family in Heidelberg. This was a chance to try something different. I'm intrigued at lecturing at a new university, as well. Vilnian is only ten years old, is it not?"

"Indeed." Edmundas' chest puffs proudly. "I've been here since the beginning. It grows in bounds and is shaping up to be an exceptionally fine institution. And professors of your caliber only serve to prop it up further."

I'm spared demurring to this compliment by Edmundas' wave toward a door down a cobbled side street.

"Is this your dwelling?" I look up with interest. Shutters frame windows that glow with the warmth of candlelight. It's one of a connected row of houses, but the solid stone and finely wrought iron balconies of the second floors speak to the wealth of their inhabitants.

"Yes. It's closely situated to the halls of study. Please, come this way."

Edmundas leads me to the entryway and opens the door. A servant bustles forward to take our overcoats and hats. She is closely followed by a well-dressed woman whose graying hair is wound in fashionably braided buns on either side of her head. She smiles at us.

"And who is this, my dear Mykolas?" she asks in a low, pleasant voice. "You told me to expect visitors, but I am in the dark as to their identity."

"This is Menno Lenz, my dear," he says. I give a bow and she curtsies. "Master Lenz, this is my wife Mrs. Edmundas."

"It's a pleasure to meet you," I say smoothly. She nods then turns her head when two figures emerge from a side room. A boy of about eight barrels into Edmundas, who exhales at the force with a laugh.

Another figure follows more sedately but with a spring in her step that indicates liveliness. Bright eyes are framed in a heart-shaped face of youthful beauty, and peacock blue strands frame her loveliness.

"My son, Stasys," Edmundas says with a fond chuckle. He ruffles the boy's hair with good humor. "And my daughter,

Maria. She looks like a proper young lady, but she can debate philosophy with the best of my students."

Maria looks down demurely, but when she glances up, the intelligence in her eyes is plain to see.

"Enchanted, Miss Maria," I say with a bow. "And what do you prefer to study? Philosophy is a wide topic, filled with epistemology, metaphysics, ethics, aesthetics…"

"Humanism interests me the most," she says in a clear voice. "I read much of Petrarch. I find the notion intriguing that we might find greater truth by returning to the letters of the ancients for illumination."

"Seat me next to your admirable daughter, if you will," I say to Edmundas with a smile. "I should like to hear her defense of Petrarch."

The market is noisy with hawkers, children shouting, and shoppers arguing prices in the Mozarabic dialect of Al-Andalus. The scents of Arabic cardamom and turmeric mingle with Spanish garlic and oregano, a pleasing combination in the eleventh-century city of Toledo under Umayyad rule.

The market today is strung with blue and gold banners in preparation for the festivities tonight. A local lord is marrying a princess from the north, and to celebrate his good fortune he has rashly promised libations for the neighborhood. I expect he doesn't know how fast word traveled about the impromptu party tonight.

I'm helping corral poultry in exchange for the ride the chicken seller gave me in his cart to the city. At sunset I will be free to wander and explore as I will, but until then the chickens and I glare at each other, their beady eyes and sharp

214

beaks promising retribution should I attempt to wrestle them into submission.

"Merlo!" the chicken seller calls. "One fattened hen for this fine gentleman."

I eye the flock in their wooden crate to find the least aggressive bird. Their heads bob in anxiety. With a darting motion, I grasp a nearby bird by the neck.

If done properly, one swift twist of my wrist will result in a broken neck and a chicken ready to pass to a customer. This time, I don't do it properly. Before I can flick my wrist, a beak like a knife stabs my fingers with vicious glee.

"Ah!" I grunt with pain. Feathers flap everywhere, and I could swear that the chicken suddenly grew four extra wings. I attempt to wrap my arms around the panicked bird, and eventually manage to subdue the animal.

In the relative peace of a moment, my eyes flick around to see who might have watched my debacle. A pair of inquisitive brown eyes surrounded by sky blue lauvan observe me merrily. The girl's hands are deep in a barrel of shiny silver trout, and scales fleck her bare arms.

I can't help my grin. We are both in such ridiculous states that it's all I can do. She answers with a brilliant smile of her own, and I resolve to seek out the golden cheeked beauty as soon as I am released from my duties.

I bought my fishing boat for a song from a grateful fisherman after I fixed the roof of his cabin outside Regensburg in fourteenth-century Bavaria. He had two vessels, after all, and this one is the worse for wear. With my skills, it didn't take much to patch it up well enough.

Now, I drift down the Danube river, whistling. The sun shines and the water sparkles. I have no set destination, so we will see where the river takes me. With the boat, I can easily fish for my supper.

The river bends around a pleasing cluster of willows and widens. Dotted along the edge of the expansion are huts of a hamlet, mostly visible from trails of smoke from cooking fires.

I sigh in contentment. Although I don't know where I'm going, nor for how long, it's a beautiful day on a picturesque lake. Enjoying the moment is a skill I have acquired over the years.

Soft notes of a woman singing reach my ears. I sit up and scan the shore. She has a clear, high voice that carries hauntingly over the lapping waves, and I yearn to see the creator of the song.

Before long, a woman appears through a gap in the rushes. Her blond hair glints in the sun above her undyed woolen tunic that is tucked into her belt so that it hangs above the knee. It must be laundry day, for she scrubs at a tunic in the water while she sings. It's a folk song that I know well, and when she finishes one verse, I start on the next with a hearty tenor.

Her head snaps up and she watches me with eyes crinkled in amusement. When I finish the verse, she stands straight with her hands on her hips.

"Hello, stranger," she calls out. "Passing through?"

"The name's Marian," I say with a smile. "And I might pass through, I might not. Is this your village? How far is the local market?"

"This is my home," she says and picks up the tunic to wring it out. "The market at Straubing is only a half-hour's walk away." She looks at me coyly. "And I'm Gretchen."

"Do you think they would want fish at this market of yours? I have a way with the net."

216

It's not the smoothest line, but Gretchen laughs with true mirth. It's an infectious laugh, and my mouth pulls up in an involuntary grin.

"Come, sell your fish at the market," she says and brings her laundry basket to her hip. "And then sing with me some more."

CHAPTER XXV

The night is cold and dark when I wake from restless dreams of meeting Minnie through the ages. Although the memories left me in a curious state of hope, the oppressive darkness and the heavy knowledge of Minnie's death threatens to push me into the floor with their weight. I take a deep breath which catches in my throat.

The sound must carry to the living room, for Jen appears in my bedroom door from her nest on the couch.

"Merry?" she whispers. "Are you awake? Are you okay?"

I shake my head, unwilling to force words through my tight throat. She must see movement, for she comes forward to sit on the edge of the bed.

"Do you want company?" she says.

"Yes," I croak. I hate this time of night. I'm afraid to go to sleep and see my love once more, and I'm more afraid to stay awake and see the emptiness where she should be.

Jen lifts the covers and slides under. She lies at an angle so our bodies do not touch, but she rests her head on my outstretched arm. The comforting weight compels a sigh from me.

"That's as close as I'm getting," she says. "I remember what you wear to bed."

Despite myself, the comment forces a weak chuckle from me. Jen once ripped the covers off and was horrified to find I sleep in the buff.

"Fret not, I wore bottoms in your honor tonight."

Jen laughs lightly and wriggles a little to get comfortable.

"You'd better not snore," she says, but I'm already drifting. Her warm weight in the bed convinces me that I'm not alone. This time is not like the others. Minnie might be gone, but my friends are still here, as they always have been.

In the morning, my bed is empty but there are quiet rustlings coming from the kitchen. I try to pretend that Minnie is preparing breakfast, but the knot in my gut reminds me of the truth. To avoid thinking about it, I rise and pull a shirt over my head with a soft groan—I didn't heal my bruises last night, only my broken arm—then walk to the kitchen.

Jen stands in front of the counter with two mugs. She jumps when she sees me.

"Sorry, Merry, I didn't mean to wake you."

"It's fine." I lean against the counter and accept the mug Jen passes to me. The heaviness of the night is less, now that the sun is up and I am not alone. Jen searches my face.

"How are you this morning?" she asks tentatively. I sigh and swirl the coffee in my mug as I think. My hand reaches for a lauvan knot on my hip and I absentmindedly massage it with my fingers.

"Sore and achy from being filled with the power of the earth fundamental. I don't think I was stretched enough." I run my hand through my hair and get stuck in a splotch of mud. "Not to mention the battle bruises. Also, dirty. Did I really not shower last night?"

"There were other things on your mind," Jen says quietly. I sigh.

"They still are."

We are silent for a long moment. Jen's lauvan squirm, as if she searches for something to say. I break the silence first to ease her worry.

"I'm not going to fall apart, if that is what concerns you."

She peers at me with a frown.

"No? I might, in your place."

"I have before, that's true. When Josephine died, I did literally nothing for a year, then I experimented with every new drug I could find. It was the eighties, and there were plenty to try. I even joined a well-known hair metal band in France and took over the lead guitarist's place when he was too high to play."

Jen covers her laugh with her hand.

"And nobody noticed?"

"There was a lot of hair and makeup going on. We were roughly the same build and coloring. No one was too picky." I sip my coffee and enjoy the warmth it brings to my cold chest. "My point is, I do tend to fall apart when my wife dies." I pause to let the squeeze in my chest subside after the hurtful words. "But this time feels different."

"How so?"

"This time, I have a reason for carrying on. Others depend on me. When you're only looking out for number one, who cares if you fall off the map for a few years? There's no accountability. Now, I don't have the leisure to fall apart, and in a way it's a relief. Needing to keep it together gives me the strength to keep it together. Does that make sense?"

"A little." Jen tilts her head to study me. "But if you need time to let go, take it, okay? I'm here to help, and so are the others. Don't feel like you have to shoulder everything alone."

I put down my cup and gather Jen in my arms. She's not Minnie, but it's comforting to embrace someone. She clutches me back.

"Thanks, Jen," I say when I release her. "Now, get out of here. You've done your time for today. Go clean yourself up. You look like you've been rolling in a pigpen."

Jen rolls her eyes at me.

"Take a look in the mirror."

Once Jen has been reassured that I'll be all right on my own, she leaves with a parting admonishment for me to call if I need her. I close the door behind her and let the quiet of the apartment surround me.

I walk slowly around the empty apartment, letting myself see traces of Minnie: the novel she was in the middle of reading and now will never finish; her sweater draped over a dining room chair; a box of her favorite brand of tea in the kitchen; her makeup and shampoo in the bathroom. I breathe deeply, allowing myself to fully feel the loss of my wife, the regret for the time we will never have together, and the sadness for a young life cut too short. Tears drip down my cheeks, but I don't break down.

The one component that is missing from this all-too familiar post-death ritual is loneliness. I am not alone. If I need someone to talk to, to distract me, to listen to my memories, or to simply sit with me, I have someone to call. And not just anyone. I have the people who have followed me my whole life, who have been there with me through everything, and who will continue to be there. And that is a comfort that I have never had in the past.

Grief is there, huge and unyielding, but it is a familiar demon on my back. Since loneliness doesn't sit on my other shoulder, the grief is easier to bear.

I wipe my face with the back of my hand and wander to the table. The personality tests that Minnie gave me are spread there, half-filled out with my careless scrawl. I tidy them into a neat pile.

I have direction now. I don't need a test to tell me my next move. The elemental world needs me, and I intend to fulfill my fundamental duties with a zeal that Xenia never showed. The thought fills me with purpose, which is something I have never felt upon the death of a loved one. I embrace the sensation. If I can't have Minnie, then I will plunge into this whole new world while I wait for her to return to me.

And she will. She always does. I'm counting on it.

After I have showered, changed, and healed the last of my bruises, there is a knock on the door which surprises me. I thought Jen would have told the others to leave me alone for the rest of the morning.

The door swings open to reveal Cecil. His pained look confuses me.

"Cecil. Did you have need of healing? I'm sorry I didn't offer last night."

"No, no, I'm fine," he says and twists his hands together. "I'm sorry about Minnie, and I'm sorry to disturb you, after everything yesterday. It's just—I can't do this anymore. Please, I want to forget. I want to be normal again, never knowing that the elemental world exists, never knowing about Jen and Alejandro and all that. Please, Merry, I've thought a lot about it, and I want this."

"All right," I say, and Cecil looks taken aback. "It's your life, and your choice. I will miss you—you've been a loyal friend and a staunch ally—but I understand. Come in, sit down."

Cecil wanders past me into the living room. He still looks bewildered by my acquiescence.

"Okay, then." He digs into his pocket and extracts two envelopes. "Can you give these to Jen and Alejandro?" He swallows. "After I forget?"

"Of course." I take the envelopes and place them on the coffee table. "Sit down. This will take a minute."

Cecil perches on the edge of the couch then raises his hand.

"Wait. You know I don't mean anything by this, don't you?" He looks at me pleadingly. "It's not that you all haven't been

222

good to me. We've saved each other's necks again and again, and I owe you as much as you owe me. It's nothing to do with you and the others."

"Cecil, you don't have to explain. It's too much. I understand. Trust me, sometimes I've wished I could forget. Perhaps in your next life we will meet again, and I can wake your memories, and you can decide anew if you would like to have them back."

Cecil relaxes his shoulders, and the crease in his brow loosens.

"That's true," he murmurs. "There's always next time."

I pat his back once, then my fingers begin their work. I knot carefully this time. At the cave, I worked quickly and carelessly on the Potestas members who almost killed Minnie. My handiwork was flawed, and some people were left damaged. This time, my fingers are meticulous.

A minute later, I knot the last strand and step back. Cecil's eyes glaze over, then they focus on me in confusion.

"Sorry, who are you?" he says.

"You almost passed out," I say heartily. "Better get home and eat something, man. I assume you don't want to buy the lamp after all?"

I gesture at a lamp on the side table, pretending to be selling it on the used market. Cecil shakes his head, bemused.

"Not today. Thanks for showing it to me."

"Not a problem. Have yourself a good day." I usher him to the door. Before he leaves, I say, "See you again sometime."

Cecil looks at me, searching my face for something he can't find.

"Yeah," he says finally. "See you again."

223

Cecil's visit, while not entirely unexpected, unsettled me enough that I want company again. I plan to plug into the lauvan network this afternoon—in fact, I'm looking forward to it, both from wanting to begin my new purpose and also as a distraction from Minnie—but I have a task to complete first.

I walk down to the underground parking and stroll to my stall. When the royal blue van peeks its nose from behind a cement pillar, my feet stop on their own. My breaths shorten.

I can't do it. I can't get behind the wheel of the van I bought especially for Minnie. She wanted a Volkswagen van when she was Josephine, and I finally found her one last month and updated it at great expense. She was delighted with it, and her joyful laughter echoes in my memories.

I turn around and walk back up the stairs. Perhaps another day I can face the van, but not today. Not when the pain is so fresh and raw. It makes visiting Alejandro's even more vital.

I transform into a merlin falcon to soar to Alejandro's house and use the time to ponder Minnie's behavior over the past few days. It's easier to think of her while in a bird's body. Emotions are duller, and tears can't form. I assumed most of her odd behavior was from her emerging elemental personality, but now I wonder how much was from the knowledge of her upcoming sacrifice. The river elemental must have told her. My tiny bird's heart squeezes at the secrets Minnie bore alone.

Alejandro opens the door quickly when I knock after turning back into a human. His face is concerned and unsure, and his strands reflect the same.

"Merlo," he says quietly. "How are you?"

I shrug. There is never a good way to answer that after a death. No one is ever good, or fine, but I don't want to get into the details of my psyche. I need to tell him and the others about Minnie's sacrifice—she deserves that honor—but I can't bring myself to talk about it. I will muster my strength soon, but not today.

"I'm still here," I say. I thought I wanted company, but now I'm regretting coming. Alejandro dithers about, wondering what to say next. I spare him the consternation. "I came to get something."

I brush past Alejandro and kneel on the floor beside the round table. Liam's door is closed, and I'm relieved that I don't have to speak with him or Chloe. I'm already plotting my escape from Alejandro. He is my best friend, but I need to be alone. Is that odd? What I want is solitude with the knowledge that my friends are only a phone call away.

The grail is hanging in a small drawstring bag from a hook underneath the table. It's a shapeless form, but multicolored lauvan peek out from the bag's opening. I snatch the bag and shimmy back to a standing position.

"I'll look after this now," I announce. Alejandro's eyes flick to the grail in my hand then back to my face. He doesn't argue but merely nods.

"Of course."

I relax from the tension I didn't realize I carried. Alejandro understands. When Minnie comes back—and she will—I need to have a way to recognize her. I won't tolerate another fifteen centuries of fumbling around in the dark without her. Whatever it takes, we will be together again.

Alejandro leans against the wall and looks at me with crossed arms.

"Xenia is really gone, isn't she?"

There's a flash of Minnie's lifeless body before my eyes, midnight blue and chestnut brown strands both ripped from it.

"Yes. Yes, she is."

Alejandro heaves a tremendous sigh.

"Good. What is it like, being a fundamental? Do you still

feel like you?"

"For the most part." I rub my side where the ache of being stretched to my limit still bothers me. "I haven't entered the lauvan network since yesterday, but that's what I'm doing after this. It was bizarre, though. I could sense every part of the Earth, from pole to pole, from its conception to the present, all the phenomena that occur. It will take some getting used to."

Alejandro exhales in a laugh.

"Probably an understatement."

"Yes. I assume the elementals will show me the ropes now that I'm fully instated. They seemed eager to have a proper fundamental once more. I don't know whether my presence alone will calm the chaos, or if I will need to take a more active role. I'll find out my duties shortly. I'm looking forward to them. It gives me a reason to hang around until Minnie comes back."

I try for a half-grin which feels forced, but Alejandro smiles back with relief in his eyes.

"Good. I'll be here to bother you until then," he says, and the words ease some of the knots in my heart.

A bedroom door opens, and Liam walks out. The sound of a violin playing a melancholy tune drifts out before he shuts the door. The muffled strains filter into my psyche.

"Merry," Liam says. "You're here."

I shrug. I don't plan to be for long. Liam's eyes glance at the bag in my hand, and his eyes widen.

"Are you taking away the grail?" he asks in a constricted voice. "That's—that's fine, but before you do—" He swallows. "Can I touch it?"

I glance at Alejandro in surprise, and he returns my look with raised eyebrows. Liam came to this decision by himself.

"You're sure?" I ask. I have already erased one friend's memory today. I'm loath to do it again too soon.

Liam nods slowly.

"This isn't a snap decision. It's time. Honestly, I would have done it days ago, but Xenia took over my life and I was otherwise occupied." He wrinkles his nose at the reminder of the compulsion he was under. "I want to know one way or another."

Alejandro's lauvan dance with anticipation. My grief rests on me too heavily to mirror his emotion, but a flicker of interest nibbles at the edges. I reach into the cloth bag and extract the grail.

"You'd better sit down," I say.

Liam nods nervously and sits on the edge of a kitchen chair. I place the grail on the round table before him, then Alejandro and I both take a step back to watch. Liam stares at the grail, takes a deep breath, and touches the rim with hesitant fingers.

The now-familiar rictus grabs Liam, and Alejandro and I wait for a long minute until Liam stops shaking and the multicolored strands retreat to the grail. He drops his hand to his side with trembling fingers.

Alejandro slides into the chair next to Liam, and I prop myself on the table's edge. Liam opens his eyes but stares unseeingly at the wall opposite.

"Do you know?" Alejandro whispers. "Do you have a past?"

Liam winces, and my beleaguered heart squeezes. That motion looks suspiciously like a new memory arriving.

"I do," he says. "But it's all so jumbled. Give me a sec."

"See if you can remember Merry," Alejandro prompts. "He always turns up like a bad dime."

"Bad penny," I correct him, but the phrase makes my mouth quirk upward. "Any swords flashing around? Alejandro wants to know your earliest memories, of course. Tunics, swords, rainy hills. Men named Arthur and Gawaine. You know the sort."

Finally, Liam's eyes open. He smiles, his grin widening with every passing moment. He meets Alejandro's eager gaze.

"You called me Elian," he says.

"Elian." Alejandro sits back in his chair, looking winded. I look at Liam through narrowed eyes, sizing him up.

"That fits," I say at last. "I can see it."

"Me too," Alejandro says. His voice grows louder. "Me too. This is so great. Another one! And Elian. I can't wait to hear your other memories. I'll give you the password to Wayne's website and you can start filling it out. I wonder who else you were? Do you want to spar right now? It helps me get my memories back."

I chuckle and pat Liam's shoulder as I stand.

"I'll leave you in Alejandro's capable, enthusiastic hands. Welcome to the fold, Liam."

"Thanks, Merry." Liam looks overwhelmed, but his strands flow peacefully around him in a way they haven't since we sprang the past-lives news on him.

I place the grail in its bag and take my leave. Alejandro's happy chatter is jarring in my present mood, although I am glad for him and Liam both. It comforts me to know that another friend is by my side, even though Minnie is gone.

I fly home, although my wings feel heavier than normal. Is it a function of my new position as fundamental? Am I too earthy to stand flying? I pump my wings harder in determination. I don't care what I am. They won't take flying away from me. It's too freeing up here. I might be of earth, but I'm also half-human, and I know how to control all four elements.

It's midafternoon by the time I reach my apartment once more, and a watery sun peeks out from thin gray clouds. The storm has passed, although in Vancouver's rainy climate, I don't doubt that another one is swift on its heels.

I circle down to a patch of grass, tucked out of sight of most of the apartment's windows. The turf is soggy, but I don't care overmuch. Clothes can dry, and I have more important things to do than worry about a little damp. My fundamental duties call to me, and I am eager to answer.

Tremor and Quake respond my summons almost instantly.

"You did it," Quake says in awe.

"My fundamental," Tremor says reverently.

"Hey now, no groveling," I say. "You were my teachers, and you still need to show me the ropes. I know next to nothing about all this."

"We are happy to serve," says Tremor. "And we will show you everything you wish. Come to us another day—there is plenty of time. But, first, you must speak with the other fundamentals."

"How do I do that?" I truly am a babe in the woods. It's daunting, but a twinge of exhilaration threads through me. Finally, there is something new to explore. The wanderlust in my soul raises its sleepy head and sniffs the air in curiosity.

"The simplest way," says Quake. "Since you're in a human body, is to gather the other three elements together. They are waiting for you."

"Until tomorrow, then," I say to the two elementals and exit the network. They dwell in the earth strands, and I suppose the other fundamentals reside in their elements. How do they communicate between each other? These are things I must find out.

Water is everywhere—flowing blue strands snake through the grass—and so is air, but fire is more difficult. I snap my fingers. I don't need to be on the ground for this conversation. I am Earth, so there is no need to ground myself. My apartment will do the trick and has the added benefit of dry clothes.

Once I am changed, I set myself up in the living room with a glass of water and a lit candle. I twine blue, silver, and orange lauvan around my finger and send out my intention then wait.

Moments later, figures bloom from my hand, swaying apart until three torsos are lined in front of me, connected to their sources by thin strands.

"Earth," Water says with a fluid voice. "Welcome and thank you."

I nod, unable to say anything at this stark reminder of Minnie's sacrifice. Water was still in half-dormancy until she died.

"Did it help?" I eventually croak. The others don't appear to be in any hurry to speak. "Becoming a fundamental? Is it still chaos over there?"

"It helped," Air whispers. "There is much still to do, but already our plane is restoring itself. Your mere presence in the threads yesterday went far toward righting the wrongs, but to continue the healing, you must spend time in the earth threads."

"What does that mean?" I ask. Finally, some details are emerging. "Should I plug in every night? How much time do I need to spend there?"

"Anything will help." Fire's voice crackles and spits brightly, but I sense that it is a function of Fire's essence and not a reaction to my question.

"Whatever you can spare right now," Water says. "Eventually, you will want to spend more time there, but for now, a visit once a day will do. Spend time with the two elementals assigned for your education. I believe you call them Tremor and Quake?"

"I can do that." Relief laces my voice, and I don't try to hide it. I was concerned that I might have to spend half my time flitting about the earth network, but daily lessons are no hardship. I will need a distraction now that Minnie won't be here every evening. I swallow past the lump in my throat.

"There is one other thing," Air says. "I understand that you lost someone dear to you when you became the earth fundamental."

I nod, unable to speak.

"Because of your heritage, she has reappeared to you many times, has she not?" Air says.

"Yes. I will wait for her return like I have for centuries. It should happen eventually."

"There might be a way to bring her back sooner," Water says slowly.

My heart skips a beat.

"What?" I gasp. "I thought Xenia was only toying with me. You mean she was right?"

"No, Xenia was toying with you," Air says quickly. "She does not have the power to do that, not on her own. Elementals do not control the threads of living creatures. However, we can contact the one who does. It will take some time, but if all four of us are of one mind, we can approach and ask for a boon, if that is something you desire."

"Yes," I croak. "Yes, oh yes."

I breathe heavily. Is it possible that Minnie could be fast-tracked back to the world of the living? My hands tremble while I hold onto the elemental lauvan. I was willing to wait—not happily, but with resignation—but hope lights a fire in my chest. Minnie, my Nimue and all the rest, might be in my arms once more, sooner than I even dreamed.

"We will inquire," says Water. "And let you know what we find. In the meantime, let Quake and Tremor show you around.

You will quickly grasp what you need to do by instinct."

"Farewell," says Air.

They sink into their elements and disappear. I drop my hand and grab the bag that holds the grail. I slide it out and stare at the enameled bowl.

My purpose is clear—learn all I can about being a fundamental so I can right the balance that Xenia so carelessly wrecked—and my hope is a beacon in the night. Minnie will return to me, sooner or later.

I rub my sleeve against the grail to polish it. My new role will drive me through the dark days ahead, giving me purpose and a reason for carrying on. My reward? Minnie by my side once more.

The future holds much promise.

ALSO BY EMMA SHELFORD

Immortal Merlin
Ignition
Winded
Floodgates
Buried
Possessed
Unleashed
Worshiped
Unraveled

Magical Morgan
Daughters of Dusk

Nautilus Legends
Free Dive
Caught
Surfacing

Breenan Series
Mark of the Breenan
Garden of Last Hope
Realm of the Forgotten

ACKNOWLEDGEMENTS

Thank you for my wonderful reading team: Wendy Callendar, Dave Roche, and Gillian Brownlee. Deranged Doctor Designs produced another exciting cover. And thank you to my Fantastical Lair, who helped brainstorm with me. You're the best!

ABOUT THE AUTHOR

Emma Shelford feels that life is only complete with healthy doses of magic, history, and science. Since these aren't often found in the same place, she creates her own worlds where they happily coexist. If you catch her in person, she will eagerly discuss Lord of the Rings ad nauseam, why the ancient Sumerians are so cool, and the important role of phytoplankton in the ocean.

Emma is the author of the Nautilus Legends (a marine biologist discovers that mythical sea creatures are real), the Immortal Merlin series (Merlin is immortal, forever young, and living in the modern day), and the Breenan series (a young woman follows a mysterious stranger into an enchanting Otherworld).

Printed in Great Britain
by Amazon

32637921R00138